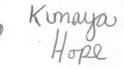

Fairest of All

A Tale of the Wicked Queen

By Serena Valentino

Autumn
Publishing

Autumn
Publishing

Published in 2019
by Autumn Publishing
Cottage Farm
Sywell
NN6 0BJ
www.igloobooks.com

Written by Serena Valentino
Adapted in part from Disney's *Snow White*

LEO002 0319
8 10 11 9 7
ISBN 978-1-78810-770-9

Printed and manufactured in China

Dedicated with love to my father,
who always told me I was beautiful,
even when I did not see it myself.
—S.V.

CHAPTER I

ROSE PETALS, KISSES AND CAKE

The apple blossom trees in the castle courtyard bloomed with the lightest of pink petals and sparkled with shimmering silver baubles, reflecting the sun brilliantly.

Garlands of wisteria and gardenia were draped over the stone well at the foot of the castle's grand staircase, which was strewn with pink and red rose petals. One hundred attendants, fitted in the finest garments of deep blue edged in silver trim, stood along the castle's main gate, ready to greet the royal wedding guests who were now starting to pour into the courtyard. It seemed the entire world was now assembled by the old well, waiting to see the king's beautiful new bride, a distinguished beauty who seemed to magically appear from legend and myth, the beautiful daughter of the renowned maker of mirrors. The courtyard was bursting with royalty from neighbouring kingdoms, all waiting for the wedding to commence.

The Queen stood alone in her chamber, staring at her reflection in the mirror, which looked back at her rather nervously. No woman could have her life so completely changed and not expect some level of anxiety. She was marrying the man she loved, becoming a mother to his daughter, and she was to be queen of these lands. Queen. She should be happy, but something about the mirror she was holding filled her with a horrid sense of dread that she could not account for.

Verona, the Queen's lady-in-waiting, cleared her throat to announce her presence and then rushed into the chamber. Verona's bright eyes, the colour of the sky, beamed with happiness. The lady glowed with a light that seemed to come straight from her core, illuminating her fair skin and glinting off her milk-and-honey hair.

The Queen smiled weakly as Verona embraced her. The Queen had never been surrounded by such beauty. Nor had she known happiness. Not until she came to this court. And now, here was a woman she loved as a sister.

Snow White followed Verona into the Queen's chambers. She was a lovely little creature of three or four with a joyous bounce in her step and an inextinguishable sparkle of happiness twinkling in her eyes. Her skin was fairer than a virgin snowfall, her tiny, pouty lips redder than the deepest ruby, with hair as black as a raven's feathers. She was like a delicate porcelain doll come to life, especially this day, in her little red silk-velvet dress.

Verona held Snow by her tiny hand, hoping it would discourage the little girl from fidgeting with the beading on her delicate dress.

"Snow, my dear, stop pulling at your beads, you'll ruin your dress before the wedding even commences."

The Queen smiled and said, "Hello my pretty little bird of a girl; you look lovely today."

Snow blushed and hid behind Verona's skirts, peeking at her stepmother.

"Doesn't your new mother look pretty today, Snow?" Verona said.

Snow nodded her head.

"Then tell her, dear," coaxed Verona as she bent down, smiling at the coy little girl.

"You look very pretty too, Momma," said Snow, melting the Queen's heart.

The Queen opened her arms to the child, and with Verona's gentle encouragement, Snow moved forward to accept the Queen's embrace. Snow was a little bird of a girl, such a lovely creature; it tugged at her stepmother's heart, as if the child's beauty hurt her deeply. As she took Snow into her arms, she was filled with a love she had never known. She thought the weight of that love might cause her heart to burst, and in a secret place buried deep within her heart she wished somehow she could absorb the beauty of this child, so she herself would truly be beautiful.

"You do look quite striking, my Queen," Verona said, smiling knowingly, as if she had seen into the Queen's insecure heart.

The Queen again examined herself in the mirror, and she saw something of her mother looking back at her. She remembered back to the day the King had remarked on their resemblance. Perhaps he was right. It was possible that she did look like her mother, but she had never seen it before now, standing there in the same wedding gown her mother had worn on her own wedding day.

The dress was of the deepest red, and somehow the years had done nothing to mute its brilliance. It was embroidered with a lavish pattern of blackbirds, and bejewelled with smoky black crystals that sparkled in the light. The Queen's heart leaped, then quickly sank. How wonderful it would have been to have her mother here with her today. How wonderful it would have been to have had her there at all.

The Queen knew her mother only from the painting that decorated her father's home. But as a child, she would stare at it, in awe of the woman's beauty, deeply in love with her, and yearning for her embrace. She would imagine this mother she never knew taking her into her arms, dancing in circles, the jewels that adorned both their dresses catching the light while they laughed.

The Queen broke away from her reverie to look at Snow, who was playing with the tassels of the curtains at the far end of the room. For all the joy in her eyes and her heart, the Queen knew the poor child's feelings of loss. There must have been an emptiness inside the girl, an inconsolable feeling.

The Queen frowned, knowing that there was nothing she could ever do to replace the King's first wife. How could Snow possibly love another woman as much as she cared for her own mother? How, especially, could she care for someone like the Queen, whose life up till now had, at best, been a string of mediocre achievements surrounded by boredom and bleakness?

As the child played and Verona tended to her, the Queen's mind drifted further, to the day she had met the King in her father's mirror shop. Her father's reputation as an expert craftsman had grown so wide, and his artisanship so well-respected, that the King himself felt it his duty to visit he who had been called the finest craftsman in all the lands.

After examining her father's wares and being gifted a mirror of his own, he was ushered outside where the Queen was fetching a bucketful of water from an old well. The King ordered his attendants to halt.

"Who is this girl?" the King asked.

"The Mirror Maker's daughter, Sire," an attendant replied.

The King made his way over to her and took her hand. She gasped, and dropped the bucket at his feet, soaking his boots right through to his stockings.

The Queen looked up nervously, expecting a harsh rebuke, perhaps even imprisonment in his dungeons. But the King simply smiled. And then he spoke to her.

She thought he was teasing her when he told her how lovely she was. That of all her father's creations, she was the finest.

"Please, don't say such things to me, Your Majesty," she said awkwardly, performing something between a curtsy and a bow as she struggled to avoid his pale blue eyes.

"And why shouldn't I? You must be the fairest maiden in this land. Nay, surely you are fairest in *all* the lands I have ever known. It is no wonder your father makes mirrors to reflect your beauty."

The Queen had struggled not to look into the face of the man who ruled over everything from her kingdom to the very well from which she was fetching water.

Then, as quickly as he had come, he was gone. When he ventured off, he promised a quick return. The Queen was bewildered and confused. How could the King possibly have felt this way towards her? Of all the maidens in the land.

Her.

The Queen's father smirked. "Clearly you have

bewitched him, daughter," he said as the Queen watched the King's convoy ride off, disappearing as it dipped below a hill, only to re-emerge on the next incline, seemingly smaller and certainly farther away.

She sat in her small, spare room that evening, gazing out her window at the star-speckled sky. Could the King be thinking of her this night? she mused as she gazed at the stars, imagining her mother looking over her, flying through the darkness; the jewels of her dress sparkling, camouflaging her among the blanket of celestial lights that twinkled in the night sky. She imagined that she was flying alongside her mother, gazing at dying suns and seeing others burst to life. She was surrounded by luminescent stardust, floating in darkness dotted with brilliant iridescence. It was the memory of the King that brought her back to her humble room.

She was sure he wouldn't come back for her.

Soon after the King's departure, the Queen suffered a new loss, her father.

In the days following her father's death, her own life was infused with light. It was as though in leaving this world, he brought all darkness with him and left her in a place where she might be able to find, if not love and happiness, at least something more than she had had up till now.

On the day her father died, before word had travelled to the King or anyone else in the land, the Queen brought every one of his mirrors out into the light. She hung the smaller ones from a giant maple tree on their grounds. It was remarkable. The mirrors swayed in the breeze, catching the sunlight and reflecting it in the most magnificent and unusual ways. Rays and beams of light danced upon the maple leaves. Reflections, like tiny playful sprites, dotted the house and the grounds.

Soon, travellers from far and wide came to see the beautiful tribute she was making to her father.

Including the King.

"Your eyes are sparkling brilliantly in the light reflected from your father's mirrors," said the King, standing under a dazzling sun.

The bright light was shining into her dark eyes, turning them a light caramel colour. The King told her she was enchanting. A terror seized her. *Enchanting*. What if her beauty were just that, as her father had claimed, an enchantment? Should she deceive such a kind, loving man? Or was it possible that she really possessed some kind of beauty?

The King made his way inside her house, and unsure of what to do, she followed him.

"Is this a portrait of you?" the King asked, looking at the only decoration in the living space of the tiny home.

"That was my mother, Sire. I never knew her."

"The resemblance is uncanny."

"I wish I were as beautiful as she was."

"You look almost exactly like her. You must see it."

The Queen just looked at the portrait in wonderment, wishing his words were sincere, but unable to take them as anything but flattery from someone who must have needed something from her. Her father's estate perhaps? The remaining mirrors? Whatever it was that the King wanted, it could not have been her.

But over time, and many visits, it seemed that she *was* all that the King wanted. Her life began to seem like a dream: light, ethereal and breathtaking. The King's people embraced her. Around fires to the melody of a minstrel's harp, the entire kingdom, and even beyond, sang of the beautiful daughter of the renowned maker of mirrors, who had stolen the heart of the King.

Verona interrupted the Queen's thoughts, bringing her back to the present. "The court, in fact, the *kingdom*, is filled with throngs wishing to glimpse their new Queen. We had best make our way."

The Queen smiled.

"And what a fine trio we will make walking in procession," she remarked as she took Verona and Snow by the hands and proceeded to the wedding celebration.

Verona had not exaggerated. Huge crowds were gathered outside, and the Queen could see this through the small windows that dotted the wall as she descended the spiral stairway. Among the crowd, the Queen recognised the King's most beloved uncle, Marcus, who caught a glimpse of her through the window and smiled. He was a large man, unkempt and jolly-looking. The Queen remembered that his wife, Vivian, had recently fallen ill. And yet, he was here for his nephew. He was standing with his dear friend, the court's Huntsman, who was a handsome man, well built with dark eyes, hair and beard.

There were kings and consorts from far and wide. And the King's three strange cousins, who dressed oddly and stuck closely together. They smiled in unison and tilted their heads thoughtfully, as one. The Queen observed their weird behaviour as she passed by another window, this one shaped like a huge letter *X*.

The entire castle was warmly lit with candlelight, glowing and ethereal, conjuring images of the Queen's favourite holiday, the winter solstice. There were so many candles lit that the room felt hot.

Too hot. The Queen's face flushed and her head spun. Her heart pounded as she walked down the aisle towards her King. He waited by the old well, which he had ordered moved from the Mirror Maker's home to the castle courtyard, so that he might always be reminded of where he first saw the Queen.

With Verona's help, the Queen steadied herself and focused her attention on her King, who was smiling brilliantly. He was beautiful, but even more so in his formal attire, with his dark hair and pale eyes. His glistening sword hung at his side, and his tall boots shined in the candlelight.

The Queen felt as if she were floating in a dream. Women with faces painted white as sheets and cheeks and lips the colours of red roses were peering at her as she glided past them. She attempted not to read the looks on their faces, instead focusing her gaze on her bridegroom.

But surely they were smiling condescendingly at her as she passed, some of them with little bundles of jasmine in their hands, the scent intoxicating and slightly overwhelming. Not only would they be jealous of her marriage, but they would also think, why her? Of all the ladies in the kingdom, why this peasant girl? There would be whispers accusing her of enchantment and evil eyes cursing her.

She finally reached the King, who stood by the well, and he took her by the hand. Perhaps he sensed her dizziness and her buckling knees. But her heart finally slowed its pounding when she locked eyes with him. The ceremony began. Verona and Snow stood off to the side. The officiant stepped forward. The King and Queen exchanged words of love, promises, rings and finally, a kiss.

Bliss.

The crowd erupted into cheers, and had the King not caught her, the Queen would have collapsed. There was a flurry, then a shower of pink rose petals illuminated by shafts of light streaming through stained-glass windows, casting an unearthly charm over the entire castle. She was in love. Beautiful. The Queen.

Everyone she encountered remarked on her beauty. She tried not to let their compliments confound her. But when she thought of it, it made her already dizzied head swim. The day whirled by in a pink haze. Her hand must have been kissed a thousand times, and she never danced so much in her entire life, not even as a child with her Nanny.

Oh, Nanny. How she wished she were here to see her on this day. She remembered something Nanny had told her in her father's kitchen one sun-drenched morning while eating strawberries and cream.

"You are beautiful, my dear, truly. Do not ever forget that, even if I am not here to remind you."

"Not here? But where would you go?"

"To dance with your mother in the heavens, dear. One day you will join us, but not for many years to come."

"No, Nanny, stay here and dance with me now! I don't want you to leave. Not ever!" And so they danced, spinning in circles, laughing and enjoying the sun streaming through the windows. That was one of the many ways Nanny would cheer her spirits: strawberries, cream and dance.

She must do that with Snow soon. The thought of it made her feel light and protected. She would be happy with the King and his beautiful, delicate little flower of a girl. She would make the child her own daughter and love her. She would tell her how beautiful she was every day of her life, and they would dance together and laugh like mother and daughter. They would *be* mother and daughter.

She walked to the edge of the ballroom floor where Snow and Verona were standing as they watched all the lords and ladies dance in circles, like blossoms floating on a lovely summer's breeze. The Queen scooped the child up, took her into her arms, and brought her into the colourful swirl of ladies' dresses. She danced with the girl, pressing her tightly against her chest, feeling that surge of love again as they danced in what seemed to be a living garden of colour and sound.

The King joined them, and the new family laughed until the early morning hours, long after the final guests had departed or retired to their rooms within the castle.

Exhausted and giddy after many hours of feasting and dance, the King and Queen took their sleeping girl to her bedchamber.

"Good night, little bird," said the Queen as she kissed Snow.

The girl's cheek felt as soft as silk on the Queen's lips. She left the child to her dreams. She was sure they were filled with lovely ladies spinning in circles and colourful dresses and banners swirling all around her.

The King took his new wife by the hand and led her to their chamber. The sun, now coming through their curtains, was casting an otherworldly glow. They stood there for a moment looking at each other.

Bliss.

"I see you have opened my gift," the King said looking at the mirror.

The mirror was oval-shaped and beautifully ornate, gilded, with serpentine designs around the perimeter, and crowned with an engraving of a headpiece fit for a Queen. It was nearly perfect. But something about it made her feel that same uneasiness that had shaken her before the ceremony. Her chest tightened and the room suddenly felt oppressively confining.

"What is the matter, my love?" the King asked.

The Queen moved to speak, but she could not.

"You don't like it?" he asked, looking crest-fallen.

"No, my love, it… I'm just… tired. So tired," she finally muttered. But she couldn't take her eyes off of the mirror.

The King took her by the shoulders and drew her close to him, kissing her.

"Of course you're exhausted, my love. It's been a terribly long day."

She returned his kiss, attempting to banish all fear from her heart.

She was in love. Bliss. And she would allow nothing to ruin this day.

CHAPTER II

DRAGONS
AND KNIGHTS

On the fourth night after the wedding, the Queen finally had her little family to herself. Lingering wedding guests and extended family had made their way back to their own kingdoms. The Queen had just said her goodbye to the King's great-uncle Marcus that morning after breakfast. He was a funny man, as wide as he was tall. Stocky, sturdy and well-built for a man his age. He was kind and clearly loved his nephew, so she couldn't begrudge him the extra time at the castle. The King, along with his uncle and the castle's Huntsman, had spent days in the forest hunting fowl and game for the evening's banquets.

"You may never see me again, my girl," Uncle Marcus had said, as he bid the Queen farewell. "I venture south in pursuit of dragons! It's a risky business, swamp dragons, but not quite as dangerous as cave dragons, I do swear to you! Did I ever recount my encounter with the great sapphire beast? The most beautiful and deadly creature I've ever stalked? She nearly burned my beard right off!"

Uncle Marcus was very animated when he spoke of dragons; he would gesticulate wildly, and re-enacted the singeing of his beard.

"And what does Lady Aunt Vivian think of your adventures, Uncle?" the Queen asked.

"Oh, she has wild notions indeed!" he said.

"Does she? And what might those be?" the Queen asked.

"She thinks it's all fancy. Can you imagine? Fancy, indeed! She thinks I'm fearful of becoming idle and bored in her company!"

The Queen laughed again. She had come to love

this man and his wild tales of dragons lurking in damp caves and his grand campaigns to steal their treasures.

"Well, I'm nevertheless sorry she was unable to attend the wedding, Uncle. We must have her to visit as soon as she is well enough to travel."

"Oh, you can be sure your aunt Vivian will swoop down on you in no time. She'll take over the house, I gather."

The Queen was sorry to see him leave. But she was happy to have her husband and daughter to herself, even if the castle seemed almost too quiet after so many festivities.

She arranged for a family dinner in one of the smaller dining halls. The Queen preferred the smaller rooms of the castle. They made her feel more at home. She wasn't a Queen here. She was a wife and mother. She was herself.

The stone walls were covered in lavish tapestries depicting images of knights in battle or lovely maidens gazing at their own beauty in reflective ponds. The fireplace was the grandest focus of the room. It was twice as tall as any man, and decorated with the face of a woman carved from the finest white stone, her eyes, downcast and serene, made the room feel protected. The warm fire made the dining hall feel cosy. The Queen sometimes wondered if the white stone beauty had been modelled after the King's former wife, Snow White's mother. She wondered if she were there to watch over the household, watch over the *Queen*, to ensure she was a worthy mother and spouse. The Queen never asked her husband, for fear of slicing open his old wounds. He had loved Snow's mother dearly, the Queen knew that, and she did her best to convince herself that it didn't diminish his love for her.

Before dinner the King gave the Queen a small box filled with his first wife's writings. The box was ornately carved with a heart and a sword lock. And the King told the Queen that it had once contained his first wife's meagre dowry. "When she knew she was dying, Rose decided to document her life so Snow might know her a little," he whispered to the

Queen, "I want you to share these with Snow when you think she is ready."

It warmed her heart that her husband should trust her with this task. But it troubled her as well. Would she be capable of it? Could she take on such a responsibility? And what if Snow fell so deeply in love with her mother through her letters that she began to resent the Queen?

"Of course," the Queen said.

Tonight the Queen wore a simple and elegant empire-waist gown of deep red, edged with black ribbons. Her long dark hair was pulled high on her head in a circlet of braids intertwined with red ribbons and jewels, and her dark eyes sparkled in the firelight as she smiled at the sight of her daughter walking into the hall hand in hand with the King. Snow was wearing a deep blue dress, which brought out the rosy colour in her plump little cheeks. The King was wearing one of his less formal, but still handsome, tunics of black, edged with gold finery.

"Ah. My love," the King said, smiling as he

entered the chamber.

The new family sat down to a fine meal of baked rosemary bread, sweet butter, hearty cheeses, roasted pork and sweet potatoes smothered in garlic and olive oil.

"I miss Great-uncle Marcus!" Snow said between bites of bread soaked in gravy.

The Queen had cut Snow's bread into interesting shapes, soaking them in gravy in hopes of inspiring the girl's appetite. Snow was a finicky eater.

"Come now, little bird, will you have no pork?" urged the Queen.

"I feel bad for the piggy, Momma," said Snow.

"Very well, my girl," the Queen sighed.

"What do you miss most about your uncle, Snow?" her father asked.

"I want to hear more about dragons, Papa," Snow said, her eyes lighting up, as she straightened her back and pretended to be one of the rare breed of ice-breathers Uncle Marcus had spoken about.

The King smiled mischievously. "Oh do you? Well, perhaps we should play a game of dragons and knights then."

Snow jumped from her seat, knocking it over, and bolted to the farthest end of the hall.

"Try to catch me, dragon!" the King shouted as he stood upon his chair and with a giant roar jumped off and tore after his daughter as she screamed with peals of laughter. He gathered her into his arms and smothered her with kisses.

"Save me, Momma! The dragon is getting me!"

The Queen laughed. She considered the gorgeous stone woman. She was gazing at her, smiling down upon all of them. The Queen felt this shower of approval, and it made her happier than she'd often been.

"Shall I have the servants bring our desserts to the morning room? We can sit by the fire and tell stories until bedtime, if you'd like," the Queen said.

"Oh yes!" said Snow. The dining hall might have been homey, but the morning room was cosier still. There were many cushions and warm furs laid before the fire. The walls were constructed mainly of paned glass, and the doors opened onto a lovely garden filled with beautiful flowers in shades of pink, red and purple. During night-time hours it was lit with candles and torches.

The three snuggled together in the morning room eating strawberries and cream. A storm had stirred up and rain pelted the windows. Snow's eyes looked heavy, and the King told her it was time for bed.

"No, Papa! Just one more story, please!" Snow pleaded.

"I've no stories left in me this night, child. We'll continue tomorrow."

"Momma, *you* tell me a story about dragons, please."

The Queen looked at her husband nervously. The King shrugged.

Unable to deny her little bird anything, the Queen put aside her inhibitions and complied: "Once, a very long time ago, a sad, lonely and greatly misperceived woman enchanted a young princess into a deep sleep for her own safety…"

"Why was she sad, Momma?" Snow interrupted.

The Queen thought about it for a moment

and said, "I think it was because no one loved her."

"Why?" asked the child.

"Because she didn't love herself. She feared rejection because she was so unlike anyone she'd ever known. She was so full of fear that she sequestered herself away. This sad woman's only companions were striking blackbirds that soared in the skies around her home, perching in trees and on ledges, gathering information so she would have news of the outside world. That is how she learned of the princess's christening. No one understood why the woman was so angry for not being invited to the christening. But you see, my little bird, she knew something the girl's parents and fairy godmothers did not."

"I thought you were going to tell me a story about dragons, Momma," Snow interrupted again.

"I am, my dear. For you see this was no ordinary woman, she could turn into a dragon, and when she did, she was a fierce, frightening creature."

"Really?" Snow's eyes were closing, heavy with tiredness.

"Indeed, but we are getting ahead of the story…"

Before she could continue the tale, Snow had fallen asleep in her arms. The King took his wife by the hand and looked at her tenderly. The firelight flickered upon his face, transforming him from a King into something more like an angel.

"You have already become a mother to her. And I adore you all the more for that.

"I'm sorry to be away from you so soon after our guests have left, my love," he said with a sincere gaze.

"Away?" the Queen asked, taken aback.

"My Queen, I am not a King who sends my men off to die in battle without sharing in that risk. If we are fighting for something, some worthy cause, then it should be worth my life as much as the lives of my men."

The Queen thought this was an honourable and valiant ethic. But it did not alter the fact that the thought of her husband out on the battlefield paralysed her with terror. And how could it be that he would rather be in battle with his life on the line, when he was King and could choose to be home with her? Was he choosing his duty over his love for her? And shouldn't she and Snow be paramount in his life? And then, a more worrisome thought entered her mind. Perhaps his loving words to her since his courtship had been untrue and he wanted nothing more than to escape her, even if it meant certain death.

"We will have to make the most of our time together, then," she said, crestfallen.

"And what will you do while I am away? How will you spend your days?" he asked.

"I think I will take Snow to the forest to pick wildflowers. And if you do not object, I would like the child to visit her mother's grave."

The King fell silent. His eyes welled up. It was strange to see such a great man, still with stony countenance, dissolve into such a state.

"I'm sorry, did I overstep...?" the Queen began.

"No, love, you did not. It means so much to me that you should want Snow to know of her mother. You are a remarkable woman. You have a beautiful heart, my darling. And I love you more than you will ever know." The Queen kissed the King on the cheek and stepped away from him.

"And I, you. We will anxiously await your return."

CHAPTER III

MIRROR, MIRROR

The Queen spent the following months further acquainting herself with her new home. With the King away, Snow occupied much of the Queen's time. The two picnicked in the woods, and the Queen taught the child delicate needlepoint. She told her tales of dragons while they snuggled by the warm fire in the Queen's chamber, where Snow slept while the King was deployed.

The two also spent many sunny afternoons visiting Snow's mother's grave site. The mausoleum was surrounded by a lovely overgrown garden filled with creeping roses, wisteria, jasmine, honeysuckle and gardenia, all favourites of the King's first wife. The scent was almost intoxicating. The Queen would sit with Snow for hours, telling her the stories of her mother that she had learned from the letters the King had brought her, and reading some aloud.

"Was my first mother very pretty?" Snow asked.

"I believe she was, my dearest. I shall ask your father if there are any portraits I may show you. I'm sure she was very beautiful."

Snow looked distressed.

"What is it darling?"

Snow cocked her head like a little rabbit might at hearing a noise. It warmed the Queen's heart.

"Well, Momma, how can you be *sure* she was beautiful?"

The Queen smiled at the precocious child.

"Well, my little bird, you are the most beautiful creature I have even seen, and so it only stands to reason…"

Snow seemed contented with this deduction.

"Tell me more about her, please, Momma. What was her favourite colour? What was her favourite dessert?"

"I'm not sure, Snow, she may speak of these things in her missives. But I do know she was a very capable horsewoman. She adored horses and hoped to teach you how to ride when you were old enough. Shall I teach you to ride, little bird?"

"Oh yes, Momma! I love horses!"

"Do you? I hadn't known."

"What's *your* favourite colour, Momma? Is it red? I think it must be red, you wear it so often."

"Yes, you're right, little bird."

"And mine, Momma? Do you know?"

"I think... blue."

"Yes, Momma!"

"Shall we pick some flowers to take back to the castle? It looks as if it may rain soon. We should venture home before we get soaked through."

"Yes, Momma. Let's pick flowers. *Red* and *blue* flowers!"

They gathered flowers as it began to rain. They

arrived at the castle steps soaked indeed, little sprigs of flowers in the folds of their skirts. But they were happy, and their soaked clothes did little to dampen their moods.

Verona was waiting for them when they arrived back at the castle, both laughing with the giddiness of the day.

"My gods! Look at you both! You're wet to the bone. You had best get out of these wet things. I have hot baths ready. Hurry along," Verona said, taking the flowers from the rain-drenched beauties.

"Will you float the flowers in bowls of water and distribute them around the castle, Verona?" the Queen requested. The Queen thought having the castle filled with Snow's mother's favourite fragrances might make it feel as if her mother were near her. How the Queen wished she knew where her own mother was laid to rest.

"Of course, my Queen," Verona answered. Then she ushered her into the Queen's chamber where her bath had been prepared.

The Queen spent most of her time in one remote

part of the room where she could settle into what she was sure was the most comfortable seat in the kingdom, a thronelike padded armchair upholstered with velvet cushions and plush trimmings. The chair was set near the fireplace, beside an alcove shelving her best-loved illuminated manuscripts. With her husband gone, she'd been ending most of her days there, and would do so again this evening. But first, a bath.

Verona exited, and the Queen stepped into the soothing tub. The steaming water melted a frost that seemed to cover the Queen's every bone. Despite the rain and the resulting shivers, she'd had a pleasant day with Snow.

Still, she missed the King terribly.

She mused as she watched the swirls of steam rise. The chamber was enormous. The stone walls were draped with detailed tapestries of red, gold and black that hung from ornately moulded rods set in iron brackets. The tapestries not only beautified the room, but kept the frigid chill outside.

The grand fireplace was flanked by two

enormous statues that seemed to have souls. Each portrayed a beautiful and beastly winged woman, both with faces severe and remote; their downcast eyes gazed down from a towering height.

A quiet knock upon the chamber door caused the Queen to stir.

"Verona, I presume?" the Queen said.

"It is I," Verona responded from behind the door. "My lady, I took the liberty of suggesting the cook make some of Snow's favourites for this evening's meal. The girl seems a little sullen."

The Queen didn't respond.

"She's missing her father," Verona continued, "as you are, I am sure. He has been away for several months now."

The Queen considered Verona's words for a moment, then broke her silence.

"Neither of us would thrive so well without you, Verona. We thank you and love you for that."

"Thank you, Majesty. Will you need any further assistance? More hot water? Or your bath sheet, perhaps?"

The Queen had already begun to step from her tub, wrapping herself in the huge, soft towel, which had been warmed on a small coal apparatus next to her.

"I've already emerged, my dear. You may enter," the Queen said.

As her attendant, it would have been Verona's duty to bathe the Queen. But the Queen was insistent that no one see her without a painted face and coiffed hair. Recently, however, she'd become much more comfortable with Verona, and had allowed the woman to see her without makeup and finery.

Verona shifted uncomfortably, no doubt because she knew how the Queen felt about others seeing her before she'd been made-up.

"I'm sure the King will be home soon, my lady," Verona said, while shifting little trinkets in the room, pretending to organise them though she might have just been attempting not to look upon the unpainted face of her Queen.

"In the meantime, perhaps you and Snow would

benefit from an adventure."

"Ah, do you have an escapade in mind, my sister?" the Queen asked, a slight smile creeping upon her lips.

"The Apple Blossom Festival. Your subjects would be thrilled if you were to attend. It would make for an even more rousing event to have their Queen and princess there to crown the Apple Blossom Maiden."

The Queen considered this. She was still, after all the ceremonies, festivals and attendants, not very comfortable in large crowds. She preferred to keep to herself. And then she remembered the child.

"You would join us, of course?" the Queen asked Verona.

"Indeed, my Queen," Verona said, smiling brightly and forgetting not to look upon the Queen's face.

"Let us attend, then."

"Thank you, my lady," Verona said, curtsying. "Might I be excused to make the arrangements?"

"Of course, dear. I can manage by myself," the Queen said with her back to Verona, gazing at her lady-in-waiting's face through her mirror's reflection.

But as Verona bowed out, the Queen noticed something that greatly disturbed, even terrified, her. Just as Verona had closed the chamber door and the Queen found herself alone, something appeared to move behind her in her mirror, the one the King had given to her on their wedding day. Something, perhaps someone, was inside with her. But it couldn't have been so. She surveyed the room. She was clearly alone. Verona had locked the door when she left the room, and, as was customary, locked it when she had entered. There was no chance anyone could have sneaked in. Still, she was sure she'd seen a face appear in the mirror, just over her shoulder.

She stared into the mirror and then searched the room. Anyone who had seen her would have thought she'd gone mad. But she needed to assure herself that she was indeed alone. And after thoroughly examining the room, that was the very conclusion she came to.

It must have been a trick of the light.

She settled down into her favourite chair to calm her racing heart. The heat from the fire soothed her, and she ran her naked toes over the bearskin rug at her feet. She must be losing her mind from sorrow. She wished she knew when, *if*, her husband would return.

Her eyes became heavy, and she began to drift off. But she was not able to sleep, still unsure that she was alone. She stood up and again walked over to the mirror. Just one last look. One more glance and then she would be able to settle down. She leaned into the mirror to examine it more closely. Perhaps it had been rigged, or charmed.

"Good evening my Queen."

The Queen attempted to scream, but could not usher a sound from her constricted throat. She instinctually swiped at the huge mirror and batted it off the stone wall. The mirror crashed to the marble floor. But for a moment the Queen was sure she'd glimpsed the shattered countenance of a man's face looking up at her through the mirrored shards, his face cracked and broken. Then he faded away as quickly as he'd appeared.

"Your Highness, what's happened? Are you well?" asked an attendant from behind the door. From his breathlessness, the Queen could tell he'd rushed there. The Queen attempted to catch her own breath.

"I am quite well, thank you. I've simply broken a mirror," answered the Queen, feeling a bit light-headed.

"Very well," the attendant said. "We will clear that away."

As the attendant began to walk away the Queen heard him say something else. She could have sworn she heard her father's name uttered.

The attendant returned with others to clear the mess. The Queen watched as her attendants scuttled out of the room with the broken bits. Then, the cursed thing was gone.

Still, her thoughts were plagued with images of the man in the mirror as she made her way to dinner. The castle was quieter without the King's hearty laughter and childlike energy. Even the small dining hall looked imposing and empty without him. And Verona had been right, Snow did look sullen with her father away. In an attempt to cheer the child, the Queen said, "I have a surprise for you, my little bird. We're to attend the Apple Blossom Festival the day after next." Snow smiled and it looked as though the stone beauty above the fireplace smiled as well.

If the Queen could only bring herself to do the same.

CHAPTER IV

APPLE
BLOSSOMS

"Momma," Snow White asked as she, Verona and the Queen stepped into the carriage that would deliver them to the festival, "is it almost time for the leaves to change?"

"Yes, dear," the Queen replied.

Snow White looked puzzled.

"But don't the apple blossoms come out after winter?"

The Queen smiled.

"Most do, little bird. But the apple blossoms in Apple Blossom Meadow are different. No one knows for sure why they bloom in the autumn. But some say that long ago a young girl lost her way in the forest. It was late in the year, near the winter solstice, and the girl was cold, frightened and hungry. She huddled beneath a stand of apple trees in the wood, and by some strange magic, the air around her became warmer, and the trees blossomed and bore fruit. The child was warm and fed throughout the entire winter. And when the springtime came, she was found by her overjoyed parents who thought they had lost her to the cold and the frost."

Snow White thought about this for a moment. And then she sat back in the carriage and smiled.

"I wouldn't want to be apart from you and Papa, Momma. But I do love apples, and it would be so nice to eat them for an entire winter!"

The Queen and Verona looked at each other and smiled at the child's innocence.

The Queen then looked outside the carriage to notice much fanfare and anticipation in advance of her arrival.

She felt guilty for not giving the villagers

proper notice of her attendance. After all, she had announced that she would be attending the festival only two days prior. She customarily would not thrust herself upon them with so little notice, but she was desperate for a respite from the gloom of the castle.

It seemed, however, that her lack of advance notice didn't quell the villagers' excitement, and as the three beauties exited the carriage a mass of subjects with apple blossoms in hand cheered on the Queen and her party. Petals floated in the air dreamily, settling around, over and on them. The Queen noticed how striking the light pink petals looked in Snow's dark hair, and noted to herself that she should have a dress of the lightest pink made for Snow. She smiled at her subjects and then took her seat to watch the festivities. Snow munched on tarts as she looked at the many pretty young girls presenting themselves before the Queen in hopes of becoming this year's Apple Blossom Maiden.

"You're prettier than any of those girls, Momma. Don't you think, Verona?" Snow asked.

But Verona was distracted by a message that had just been delivered to her by a young porter.

The Queen noticed the letter in Verona's hands, and leaned over to ask her what it said.

Verona folded the letter. Then her face brightened. She whispered to the Queen.

"My lady, the King will be home this evening!"

"Will he? We have so much to prepare before he arrives!" The Queen wanted to rush back to the castle that very moment, but she had committed to this event, and she could not let Snow or the people of the kingdom down.

"Send a letter back with the porter to the other servants," the Queen whispered to Verona, "Tell them I wish to make the grandest holiday of the King's return."

And as the Apple Blossom Festival wound down and the Apple Blossom Maiden was chosen, it was all the Queen could do to keep her mind off her husband's return. She decided that she would arrange a magnificent feast of roasted pig, her husband's favourite, and for herself and Snow, pheasant in wine sauce with wild mushrooms. The table would sag under the weight of the platters of exquisite candied pears, glazed apricots, roasted red potatoes with rosemary and jugs of warm spiced cider and wine. Everyone in the castle would eat well in celebration of the King's return.

The Queen, unable to contain the good news any longer, told Snow of her father's return during their carriage ride home. And when they arrived back at the castle, the Great Hall was already filled with glowing candles, warm fires and friendly conversation. Snow hurried upstairs with Verona to clean up and dress for her father's arrival. The Queen, for her part, did the same, frantically scouring and perfuming herself, painting her face, doing up her hair. And all the while she wore a brilliant smile.

When she arrived at the court, Snow was already there. She looked so small and delicate sitting in her high-back chair in this great hall. Before the preparations had been completed, before the Queen could take her seat, there was a blare of horns. Snow knew what this meant, and she launched from her seat and ran towards the castle entrance. The Queen followed, her speed restricted by her formal gown.

The King burst into the hall. "So, how have my beauties been occupying their time while I've been away?" he asked. A great cheer erupted in the castle. Snow leaped into his arms, and he twirled the child around and kissed her.

He had returned from the battlegrounds a different man. The Queen noticed a scar above his right cheek. His hair was not as groomed as it normally would be, and his beard had grown rough and ragged. And it was not only his physical appearance that had changed. His eyes were weighted down with sorrow and confusion. Perhaps regret. Still, underneath, the Queen could see the bright blue sparkle that she so dearly loved.

An emotion the Queen had never before felt welled up inside her. It was something she couldn't explain, something between deep sadness and sheer ecstasy. Her lip began to quiver and she could feel the pressure of tears weighing on her eyes. She ran to the King and embraced him and the child.

"I've missed you so much," she said.

"Momma crowned the Apple Blossom Maiden! Oh, Papa, she looked so beautiful with apple blossoms in her hair!"

"Was the maiden that beautiful then?" the King asked. Snow made a sour face as if her father should have known she was talking about her mother and not the Apple Blossom Maiden, "I meant Momma, she was the prettiest girl there! She should have been the Apple Blossom Maiden!"

"Oh, I'm sure she *was* the most beautiful. It sounds as if you had lovely days without me, my dears, I'm sorry I missed them."

"That's okay, Papa! But I have had a thought. If you should make friends with dragons, Papa, then, you would be able to fly home more quickly. Or maybe you could even learn to turn *into* a dragon, like the lady from Momma's tale."

The King and Queen laughed at their daughter's sweet words, and then joined their guests who had already begun to celebrate.

Then, suddenly, an explosion rocked the castle.

Screams of terror erupted from the banquet hall and attendants scurried to find safety in any corner of the hall that looked clear.

"Snow White!" the Queen called out, unable to find the child in the panicked crowd, or through the thick smoke that was filling the room. "Snow!"

Battle cries went up from the men who had so recently returned. And they were uncannily suited and armed quicker than any man could dress himself for an ordinary day. The Queen was confounded. What was happening?

At once, the great wooden door of the hall came crashing down. The Queen screamed out, terrified of what was happening.

"Snow White!" she screamed again, but the child did not answer.

Men on horseback, dressed in royal blue, stormed the hall, but the King's men appeared to be holding them off, for now.

Then, the Queen felt a strong hand grab at her arm and pull her away. She gasped, then turned to see who had grasped her. The King! And he was holding a terrified Snow White in his arms.

"Come," he said.

The Queen felt faint, but followed as best she could.

"Who are they?" she asked her husband as he led her down one of the castle halls, where men continued to suit up for battle.

"The opposing army from our most recent battle. They must have followed us back home. I am sorry to have put you and Snow White in danger this way."

Snow continued to shake and kept her head buried in her father's shoulder, looking up occasionally to see if the men were still attacking, if smoke was still filling the halls. Shouts and battle cries echoed through the castle. As the King unlatched a dungeon door, he grabbed a torch and quickly ushered the Queen and Snow down a spiral staircase. The dungeon was damp and cold, and in the darkness the Queen had difficulty finding her footing. The King felt around the floor of the dungeon and located a trapdoor.

"Take this torch," he told the Queen. "Descend these stairs, and at the bottom you will find a small rowboat that will carry you out of the castle and to safety."

"You will be joining us!" the Queen said.

"I will protect you in the way I know best. Now take Snow and go!" the King responded, and then he ran out from the dungeon once more.

The Queen held the shaking child close, and she made her way to the boat that the King promised would be waiting. The Queen set the torch in a brace on the boat and boarded. Snow White clung to her, and the Queen found it difficult to row the boat and hold the child at the same time. But she had to! And she did.

Soon the boat was drifting out of the castle and down a small river into the marshland that surrounded the castle. A blast of cold air hit them and the Queen held Snow White close. The Queen rowed the boat into an area that was densely covered with swamp grass, and the two sat shivering among the plants as the sky lit up red and orange around them. Both the Queen and the child started each time a blast sounded.

"Momma, is Papa going to be okay?" Snow asked, through shivering teeth.

"He always is, is he not?"

But the Queen was not sure herself what would come of this night.

Soon the blasts subsided, and the land around the castle fell silent. The Queen wrapped her cape around herself and the child for warmth. Snow White drifted off to sleep, and the Queen stayed awake all night holding vigil. And then, she felt a hand on her shoulder.

The King.

"Come, my loves," he said, and they waded through the frosty swampland, and made their way back to the castle.

The halls looked a wreck, but the castle had held up well. The King told the Queen that they had fought off the invaders.

"Will they be back?" she asked.

"No," the King said confidently.

"Your Majesty!" a voice called from the far end of the hall.

"Verona!" the Queen replied, and the two women approached each other and embraced.

"I am so happy to see you well," Verona said.

"And I, you," the Queen replied.

"We suffered no casualties. None. Your husband is a fair king and warrior."

The King dropped his gaze to the ground.

"Come now, to our chamber to rest," the King said. "Verona, please take Snow White to her room and tend to her there."

"Yes, Majesty," Verona replied.

The Queen and King made their way to their chamber. The Queen could not stomach the smell of burning wood and sulphur that permeated the castle. But once she had returned to her room, the air blowing in from the grounds helped dampen the stench.

And then she noticed something far more terrible than anything that had happened the night before.

Sitting there on the mantel was the mirror she had broken, now fully repaired and intact. But how? She was not able to pull her eyes away from it. She became disoriented with confusion and terror.

"Verona wrote to inform me of the broken mirror. I was deeply saddened, so I set the kingdom's finest craftsmen to the task of repairing it. Of course even their powers pale in comparison to your father's. I meant to surprise you with its origin on our wedding day, dear heart. I thought you would like something to remind you of your father. It is his handiwork; surely you have recognised it by now."

The Queen struggled to find her voice, to make it pleasant and not full of the terror that seized her.

"Thank you, my darling. You are thoughtful," She kissed her husband and tried to banish all fear from her heart. "I'm so happy you're home, my love," she said.

The King dropped his eyes.

"You're leaving again, aren't you?"

He nodded.

"You can't! Not so soon!"

"You saw what happened last evening! The invading kingdoms might topple us at any moment if we don't drive them back. I would rather meet them away from here, where they can't harm you. I must keep you and Snow, all of us, safe."

"Keep us safe *here*!" the Queen shouted.

"My men will do that," replied the King.

"You have been gone so long I fear I may be losing my mind!"

His heart was clearly breaking.

"No, my love, you are simply tired and weary."

The Queen wanted so much to share what she had seen in the mirror with her husband. But he would think her mad, or worse, possessed by evil spirits. Still, it seemed to be the only option if she were to convince him to remain at the castle.

"I saw a man's face in that mirror you gave me, my love. He spoke to me!"

"Oh, my darling," the King said, appearing to be concerned for her sanity.

"Don't look at me that way! If you were not gone so often, I would not be plagued with such visions," she said, paralysed with panic.

"You are not going mad, my love. You are simply exhausted. You are the strongest woman I know, but even you have your limits. I want you to rest tomorrow. I will spend the day with Snow, and then you and I will have the evening to ourselves."

"I'm sorry, my love. I shouldn't have blamed you. Please, put this out of your mind, my dear. I promise you all will be well," the Queen said.

The King held the Queen tightly, and she broke down weeping in his arms. She was comforted there, and imagined that this is how a child must feel when she is being protected by her parent. Then the great Queen fell asleep in the King's arms, sobbing.

CHAPTER V

A Trick of the Light

In the days after the King's departure, the Queen began to feel more alone than she had at any point since she'd arrived at the castle. She could share her horrible nightmares with no one. It was difficult enough for her to reveal her vision to the King. If she were to mention it to anyone she trusted less, she was sure they would charge her as a witch, and have her burned at the stake.

This made the fact that she was plagued with images of the man's face all the more terrible. She thought of having the mirror removed, but that would simply arouse suspicion. She was confident that the King had written her vision off as a product of an exhausted mind. But she also knew that the others in the castle, including Verona, were aware that the mirror was a heartfelt gift from the King. How would she explain rebuking such a gift?

She decided to drape it with thick velvet curtains, hoping that keeping it out of her sight would also keep it from her mind, and prevent it from affecting her. When Verona questioned her, the Queen explained that she hoped the curtains would preserve the mirror by shielding it from the elements. A reasonable lie, which Verona accepted without question.

Still, the Queen was plagued by dreams about the man she saw in the mirror. He would smash it with his fists from within, glass shattering and flying in all directions. The Queen would bury her face in the crook of her arm as the glass sliced her. Her blood poured onto the floor, mingling with the jagged shards of glass. Sometimes in these night terrors, a man would crawl out from the mirror, grotesquely contorting his body, falling onto the ground, then grasping a large piece of broken mirror, clutching it so tightly it cut his own hand as he chased the Queen onto rocky cliffs.

She woke nightly in cold sweats, heart pounding, often to the sound of her own screaming. Some nights she woke in pain, convinced her feet were bloodied from running down stairs that were covered in broken bits of mirror, each shard reflecting a horrible image of the Queen, looking not like her beautiful self, but haggard, wart-covered and aged.

She began to wonder if demons had invaded her soul. Riddled with anxiety over the mirror and deep sadness that she did not have her husband by her side, she began to feel afraid to leave her bedchamber. Each morning, Verona would arrive with fresh rose water in hopes she could convince the Queen to get out of her nightdress.

"I promise you will feel much better if you dress for the day, my Queen. It's unhealthy to stay indoors so long. You look gaunt and haven't eaten properly for weeks now. I wish you would tell me what's troubling you."

The Queen felt stung by Verona's words. She gazed at her maidservant with hollow eyes.

"I can't, Verona. You would think me mad."

"I wouldn't dare."

The Queen desperately wanted to share her visions with someone. And next to her King, of all the people in the kingdom, she trusted Verona most. She decided that she couldn't go on any longer without sharing the vision in the mirror. If Verona betrayed her trust, the Queen would simply deny the story. After all, who would the kingdom believe... their Queen or a maidservant?

"Shortly before the King left I saw the face of a man in my mirror. He spoke to me."

"What did he say?"

The Queen was so surprised by Verona's calm reaction that she couldn't even recall now what the man had said.

"Have you seen him since?" Verona asked.

The Queen shook her head.

Verona walked over to the mirror and parted the curtains. The Queen's eyes widened in terror, but Verona cast a reassuring glance upon her. She revealed the mirror. There was nothing in it but a reflection of the room.

"See, my Queen, you have nothing to worry about. It could have been anything, a trick of the light, exhaustion; there are so many explanations."

The Queen did not know whether she should find comfort in Verona's words or fall into further trepidation. Now, the King and Verona had both dismissed her vision as an imagined threat. Did that not amount to madness?

"You, my Queen, are the boldest woman I know," Verona continued. "Now please, get out of your bed and go out into the sun with your daughter. She is frightened with her father away. You must think of her."

Verona was right, of course. Snow needed looking after.

"I don't think we need tell Snow about this, Verona."

"Of course not, my Queen. I will keep it between us. But make me a promise, the next time something weighs so heavily on your mind, please do come to me. I do hope you think of me as your friend."

"As my *sister*, sweet Verona."

The Queen rose from her bed, and as she did, she caught a glimpse of herself in the accursed mirror, tired and worn. Verona was visible in the mirror as well, as beautiful and serene as ever.

CHAPTER VI

THE ODD SISTERS

That same morning, a messenger delivered a notice that three of the King's distant cousins would arrive by the next morning. The typically even-keeled Queen was irritated by the unreasonably short notice. Why even send a messenger? Still, the King valued family above all else and made it clear that his kin were always welcome at the palace. The disjointed yet lyrical letter was composed of three different hands and was signed by three women: Lucinda, Ruby and Martha.

Though they had attended the wedding, the Queen had escaped their stares, which made her uncomfortable, and managed not to speak to them. This time, there would be no avoiding the sisters. Would they prove to be as intriguing in person as their letter had suggested they would be?

The indistinguishable triplets exited from a black horse-drawn carriage. Their long faces were painted a ghastly white, their cheeks were blushed with the brightest pin and the centre of their lips were painted a vivid red, which created a tiny bowlike effect. They resembled broken dolls, once loved but long forgotten. Their hair was glossy black streaked with white and adorned with red feathers. They looked like the oddest of beasts, and they walked in a way that brought to mind pecking birds.

Their dresses were the colour of aubergines, iridescent, changing from black to deep purple depending on the light. They were cinched tightly in the bust and waist, but overly voluminous in the skirts, creating a bell effect. Their tiny black pointed boots poked out from the bottoms of their dresses like slinking creatures seeking prey. They stood, the three of them abreast, arms linked, gazing at the Queen in that same fashion she remembered from her wedding day, when she was briefly introduced to them.

Their faces impossible to read, they looked neither pleased nor dissatisfied.

"Welcome, cousins. How was your journey? I dare say you must be exhausted after so many days of travel."

Martha spoke first, "We are quite—"

Ruby took over, "Rested, cousin—"

And Lucinda finished, "Thank you."

Verona spoke up, "Shall I show you to your rooms then, and send a girl to help you unpack? I am sure you are eager to refresh yourselves after your long excursion."

Only Lucinda answered, "Indeed."

The odd sisters tottered behind Verona, their tiny feet clicking on the stone floors as they chattered to themselves.

"I can't imagine it," said one.

"Unfathomable, really," said another. "Inconceivable!"

Verona only heard little bits of their conversation and wondered what they might be discussing. She resisted the urge to look back at them as she imagined the expressions on their faces, pinched in distaste, as if having smelled something rotten. Verona smiled weakly; the thought of the castle being inhabited by these peculiar women amused and disturbed her in tandem.

"Here we are, Lucinda, this is your room. Ruby and Martha, I have rooms for you down the other hall," Verona said.

Lucinda simply said "Not—"

Ruby continued, "Acceptable."

"No, not," Martha finished, "in the least."

"Come again?" was all Verona could muster.

The three sisters stared chillingly at Verona.

"Is there something wrong with your room, Lucinda?" Verona asked.

They responded as one, "We prefer to sleep together."

"I see, of course. I will have one of the grander chambers made ready then. In the meantime, would you like to take tea in the morning room?"

Lucinda said, "That would be—"

Ruby finished, "Lovely," and Martha thanked Verona as she took them to the morning room. The room was infused with light, and tea was set at the centre table, where Snow patiently waited to meet her cousins.

Verona motioned to the maid to rearrange the chairs so the sisters might sit together across from Snow. They nodded appreciatively to Verona as they took their seats. The scene looked like a macabre tea party hosted by a beautiful cherub and attended by overgrown dolls dressed in funerary garb.

"If you could pour, Snow, I have to see to your cousins' new room," Verona said.

Snow smiled. She liked the idea of playing the lady.

"And ladies, if you could please excuse me? I must be off," Verona said, curtsying slightly and then leaving the room.

As soon as Verona was out of sight, the sisters each put their hands on the table, clasping each other's, looking to Snow expectantly.

Snow poured the tea for her cousins, happy that she managed to do so without spilling a single drop.

"Would you like milk and sugar?" Snow asked.

"Yes, please," the sisters responded in harmony.

"So tell us, Snow—"

"How do you like—"

"Your new mother?" they asked.

"I like her very much," Snow replied.

"She isn't ever—"

"Cruel to you?"

"She doesn't lock you away—"

"To shield herself from your beauty?"

Snow was confounded. "No. Why would she do that?"

The sisters looked at each other and smiled.

"Why indeed?" they replied in unison, then broke into a cackle. "She isn't the stepmother—"

"Of fairy-tale myths then?"

"Lovely."

"Though a bit boring—"

"If you ask me."

"We hoped for—"

"Some excitement, some intrigue."

"We will make our own then!" they said together. "Yes, we will make our own." And they giggled uncontrollably, high-pitched and wickedly.

Snow laughed nervously, too. The three sisters stopped their laughter and turned their steely eyes back to Snow. They could have been statues that had been left in the wind and rain for too many years, the weather leaving cracks in their faces. Snow couldn't help but feel a little frightened of them.

"I would hide her away," said Ruby.

"As would I," said Lucinda.

"I wouldn't. I'd cut her into bits and make a potion of her."

"Oh yes, and we'd all drink her…"

"Indeed. She'd make us beautiful and young again."

"We'd need a raven's—"

"Feather and the heart of a dove—"

"Of course, and don't forget—"

And they all said, "A lock of her dead mother's hair."

Snow grasped the arms of her chair in fear. Her eyes grew wide and her lip began to quiver. She stood up and backed away from the sisters as far as she could. And then, to her great relief, Verona re-entered the morning room.

"Ladies, your room is ready. I can show you now, unless you are still enjoying your tea and cakes."

The three sisters stood as one, bowed to Snow and followed Verona to their room where their trunks were waiting for them.

The sisters surveyed the room. "Nice enough."

"Yes, this will do."

"We can unpack ourselves. You may leave."

They giggled as Snow darted past their room with her hands covering her face. Verona caught a glimpse of Snow and quickly excused herself to follow the girl, but caught some of the sisters' chatter as she left.

Lucinda said, "Do you think we should take Snow—"

"Into the forest? Yes." The sisters looked at each other with wicked smiles and took to their high-pitched laughing again.

Snow was in a panic and making little sense when she tried to recount to her mother and Verona what had happened during the tea.

"Oh, I think they were just teasing you, darling. They are rather eccentric," said the Queen.

"Wicked senses of humour if you ask me, my Queen, weaving tales of potions," Verona said, looking horrified. "Snow, did they actually say they were going to cut you into pieces?"

Snow nodded, frowning terribly.

"Well, I don't think they meant it seriously. They couldn't have. Perhaps Snow can dine with you tonight, Verona, so I may have dinner with these interesting ladies myself and get a gauge of their natures."

And she looked to Snow. "I will tell them, my dear, they are not to tease you so cruelly; I won't have it. Don't you worry, little bird."

Snow looked relieved.

Verona asked the Queen for a word, and the Queen obliged.

"Snow may be but a frightened child, my Queen, but I also heard the sisters talking among themselves as I left their chamber. They mentioned taking Snow into the woods. Given what Snow has already told us of them, I would advise we keep a close watch on the sisters, for I do not trust them."

The Queen sighed heavily.

"Thank you, Verona. I appreciate your loyalty and the love you have for my child."

That evening, in the smaller hall, the Queen had arranged for a splendid dinner for herself and the sisters, while Snow dined with Verona. The women ate sparingly, picking at their food like birds. They said nothing most of the evening, until Ruby broke the silence. "I fear we frightened Snow with our teasing."

Martha continued, "We can get rather carried away sometimes."

And Lucinda said, "Oh yes, we didn't mean any harm, you see."

And then they said together, "We love our little cousin."

Lucinda went on, "You see, we spend most of our time alone. We have only ourselves for company. And we divert ourselves with storytelling."

Ruby continued, "Oh yes, we get carried away at times."

Then Martha said, "We're very sorry."

The Queen smiled. "I thought as much. I'm so happy to hear this. It grieved me, the thought of having to scold three of the King's family. Now there seems to be little need for it, other than to advise you to be aware of your odd tales and stories, and not to recount them before my daughter.

"So tell me, ladies, what diversions would please you while you are here?"

The three of them answered as one, "A picnic with Snow."

The Queen laughed. "Perhaps you mean a picnic *in* the snow. It is nearly the winter!"

"Yes, but there is no better time—"

"To visit the forests—"

"Than when the trees are in their death throes—"

"And flashing their brilliant colours!"

"And if that is too cold—"

"Then there is always Apple Blossom Meadow."

A picnic? So, that is what Verona must have overheard the sisters planning when they spoke of taking the girl into the woods.

"What a wonderful idea," the Queen said, "And it can easily be arranged. I think she would love to have an outing; what a lovely day that will be. We should make a grand event of it and dress for the occasion; she will feel like a proper little lady."

Lucinda looked disappointed about something, but before the Queen could ask what, she was distracted by one of the servants coming into the room with a message on a small pewter tray.

"Excuse me, my ladies," said the Queen as she broke the letter's wax seal. Her eyes widened, her face glowed and then she burst out in elation, "Oh! This is wonderful news, indeed. I am so pleased."

She turned to the sisters. "The King will be home in a fortnight!"

The three sisters smiled and said, "In time for the winter solstice."

The Queen was puzzled. "Excuse me?" she asked.

"We assume you will keep up the traditions here in your new home," said Lucinda.

Ruby continued, "We've heard such beautiful tales of how your family made such a lovely spectacle of the holiday."

The Queen was taken aback that the odd sisters should have heard such tales of her family. But she didn't have the time to pay it any mind. The King was returning.

"I hadn't thought of celebrating in that fashion," she said. "However I think since the King is returning in time, we *should* make a festival of it. I quite like the idea. What a wonderful homecoming it would be, and he will be so pleased to have his dear cousins here, say you will stay for the festivities!"

The three odd sisters answered in tandem, through odd, wide smiles.

"Of course we will, dear."

Fairest of All

Chapter VII

Mirrors and Light

The entire castle was bustling in preparation for the winter solstice. The servants were in a tizzy making everything perfect for the King's return, and the Queen was seeing to every detail.

"I think we should have the King's favourite, of course, and then a little something more delicate for the ladies, pheasant I think, in a mushroom and wine sauce. That would be lovely, don't you think? Wonderful, and some roasted sweet potatoes with rosemary, and I think the King would come to the kitchen personally to thank you if you made your pears in brandy sauce."

The cook smiled as the Queen continued.

"And if you can manage it, a six-layered cake of chocolate, hazelnut and cream cheese; a bit rich, but we can serve anise afterwards…"

Verona came into the room looking a bit mussed, strands of her hair falling from atop her head, and her cheek smudged with what looked like ash.

"I'm sorry to interrupt you, my Queen, but I would like to discuss the decorations. I was wondering if you had anything in mind?"

The Queen looked up from the list she was going over with the cook and smiled at Verona.

"I do, actually. I have many trunks in my private chamber filled with the decorations my father made for my mother many years before I was born."

Verona looked relieved.

"How lovely, my Queen. Would you like me to start unpacking them?"

The Queen thought about it for a moment and said, "I would love your help, Verona, along with a few of our most capable maids. The mirrors will have to be washed before they are hung, of course, but I would prefer to unpack them myself, if you don't mind."

"I completely understand, my Queen."

Then the Queen looked to the cook and said, "If you'll please excuse me, I will leave with you the menu I've written up. If you have any questions, we can discuss it later this evening."

"Of course, my Queen," he responded.

And with that the Queen followed Verona to the Queen's private chamber. No one in the castle had a key to this room but the Queen and Verona. As the Queen took the key off the little belt under the fold of her blouse, she felt a tinge of nervousness. She slipped the key into the lock, turned it, then slowly opened the door.

Dread.

The room contained all of her mother's and father's things: the last of her father's mirrors, the portrait of her mother, as well as decorations that were lovingly packed away in crates, probably by her own mother's hands the year before the Queen's birth. The King had the items moved to the castle when he and the Queen were married.

She had never before had a reason to come into this room, and truth be told, she had tried to avoid it. It was full of fragments of her old life. And now, it felt as if she were stepping into a cold, dark crypt. She noticed Verona shiver too.

The Queen opened the trunk, and a rush of memory flooded over her. The trunk smelled of her father's house. It's strange how a scent can call up such vivid memories, practically transporting you back in time; the smell of the shop, the mouldy, musty scent of her former home.

She pushed the thoughts out of her mind as she unwrapped the little mirrors, noticing a face that looked much like her mother's reflecting back at her.

Verona noticed the Queen's discomfort and decided to make idle chatter.

"You look so much like your mother, I almost thought that portrait was of you."

"The King said as much when he first came to my father's shop years ago. I didn't see it then, but I do now. I almost thought she was looking back at me from these mirrors."

Verona smiled. She thought to herself how lucky Snow was to have the Queen as her stepmother. And the winter celebration would make the girl so happy. If only those horrible sisters hadn't decided to stay for the solstice. Verona felt uneasy in the sisters' presence, and wondered how the Queen did not feel the same way. Why had she invited them to stay for the celebration? Verona dreaded the sound of their rustling skirts and their chattering voices coming down the hall in the morning. Their annoying high-pitched laughs, simpering whispers and their habit of finishing each other's thoughts and sentences were far too much for Verona to bear.

She almost wished the sisters would cross the line somehow, do something that would justify the Queen's asking them to leave. One couldn't help but focus all attention upon them when they were in the room; they were like that, morbidly appealing. Verona often found herself looking at them in fascination, curiosity and revulsion, hoping her face did not betray her when the sisters caught her staring at them with a sickening awe.

Snow came into the room, interrupting Verona's thoughts.

"Lucinda says we are going to put candles and mirrors in the trees like Grandma used to on solstice eve, Momma. Is that true?"

"It is true, my little bird," the Queen said. "You may help me if you like."

Snow smiled and said, "I would love to, Momma. Let me tell my cousins I can't have tea with them and I will be right back."

The Queen noticed that Verona looked disturbed by something as she watched the girl run off.

"What is it, Verona?"

Verona made a funny pinched expression pushing her lips to the side; she looked as if she were thinking of the right words.

"Speak frankly, please, my friend. Don't censor yourself on my account."

"Well, my Queen, those sisters are rather... well, peculiar."

The Queen agreed.

"I hate to be uncharitable, but what is wrong with those women? They seem quite deranged."

The Queen could hardly stifle her giggle as she said, "I think they might have had a sheltered upbringing, and it's made them quite odd."

Verona laughed, "Sheltered indeed! Perhaps in a damp cellar?"

The Queen giggled outright.

"They look as if they've never seen the light of day."

The Queen never knew Verona to speak ill of anyone, and she loved her all the more for being so frank with her now.

"Why do they paint their faces so white? It's hideous. They look like absurd dolls brought to life by a mad alchemist!"

The Queen chuckled again. "Stop it now, Verona. You don't want Snow to hear you, she'll be back any moment now."

The two women giggled like little girls while the Queen unwrapped the solstice decorations; the mirrors reflected the light coming from the arched windows on their happy faces.

The weeks passed quickly and soon the winter solstice eve was upon them. Snow draped the grounds and the entire castle was infused with candlelight. The Queen imagined how lovely it would appear to the King as he made his way up to the castle. It must look like a magical castle from a fairy tale; a luminescent dream floating against a sea of darkness. Every tree was filled with candles reflected in the tiny mirrors hanging from the branches, casting the light beautifully, making the castle and the grounds otherworldly.

Snow White looked spellbound. It was the first time since those strange sisters arrived to court that the girl seemed to be completely at ease. The Queen wondered where the King's cousins were; they had waited a fortnight for this evening, and now they were nowhere to be found.

"Snow, do you know where your cousins are?" the Queen asked.

Snow gave her mother a weary look. "I'm sorry, Momma, but I didn't want to ruin our party."

"I think you'd better tell me, little bird," the Queen said more sternly than she had ever spoken to Snow before.

"I'm not quite sure where they are. They were acting so strangely when we went on our walk today, Momma, saying those scary things again... they chased me, yelling nasty things about my first mother and you... Then they spoke of enchanted fruit... apples that could put a little girl to sleep forever... pears that make you wither away and die... Then they said they were going to chop me up into little bits and cook me in their stew...!"

Snow's lip began to quiver, and then she burst into tears. She collapsed onto her stepmother's breast, sobbing.

"I just ran and ran until I couldn't hear them anymore, but I kept running, and when I finally looked back they weren't there. I didn't tell you because I was afraid to ruin your day."

The Queen held Snow tightly and rocked her.

"Don't worry, my darling. I will have someone

find them and have them removed from the castle. I think we should wait until after the celebration to tell your father, don't you?" The Queen motioned to Verona.

"Verona, dear, have the servants search the castle for the sisters, if they are not found, then have the Huntsman and a few of his crew go into the forest and see if they can locate them, I want them brought before me immediately. One of the men should stand guard should they return here."

"Yes, my Queen," Verona said, and she hurried up to the castle.

The Queen again turned her attention to Snow White.

"I'm so sorry. I should have never trusted those wicked women alone with you. Can you forgive me?"

"Oh, Momma, those sisters are so wicked. It wasn't your fault."

"We'll talk about this more tomorrow, my bird, but let's try to put it out of our minds for now. Look! I see your father's riding party just upon the horizon. I want him to have a wonderful homecoming, my darling. I'm just going to say this one last thing until we discuss this tomorrow. Promise me, Snow, should anything like this happen again, you come to me right away? Do you understand? I have to know you will come to me in all things, especially when someone might be trying to harm you. I am here to protect you, my sweet; no matter what, you must trust that you can always come to me."

"I will, Momma, I promise."

The Queen kissed her daughter on the cheek. She was ill at ease with the sisters for ruining this day, but for some reason could not quite muster up the anger she so desired. Perhaps it was the joy of the celebration. The Queen's father had stopped celebrating the solstice after her mother had died. How lovely it would have been to experience this as a little girl. Part of her envied Snow, really.

"Look, my darling bird, see how lovely the castle looks, your father is going to be so pleased," said the Queen in an attempt to distract the girl from her wicked cousins.

Snow looked towards the castle. Phantom

streams of light were floating through its many windows. Snow gasped.

"How is the castle doing that, Momma?" the child asked.

"A very special mirror," the Queen replied, "My father made it from bevelled pieces of glass. It's a cylinder containing a candle within that projects the shapes upon the wall."

"Oh, can I go into the ballroom and see it?" the child said excitedly.

"Of course, little bird, you can sneak in for a moment before we go into the great hall for dinner, but be sure to be quick about it."

"I will, Momma, I promise. Oh, but look, Momma, look! Father is here!"

The Queen and Snow beamed with delight when they saw the King approach. His eyes welled up with tears as he dismounted his steed and embraced them both, first kissing his wife, and then taking Snow into his arms, lifting the girl into the air and kissing each of her plump little cheeks.

"Oh, I've missed you both terribly," he said. He

again seemed different. Each time he returned from battle he was a little less himself, and a little bit more at the same time. The experience seemed to both harrow his soul and enrich his understanding of the evils the world held.

The family entered the castle together hand in hand and walked into the great hall, which was adjacent to the ballroom. Snow, remembering that her mother had granted her permission to peek into the ballroom, slipped her hand out of her father's and entered what seemed to be another world. She stood at the centre of the room near the stone table which had the mirrored cylinder perched upon it. Tilley, one of Snow's favourite ladies at court, was standing nearby, spinning the cylinder when it started to slow its cycle.

"Beautiful, isn't it?" said Tilley.

"It is!" Snow said, captivated by the images of suns, moons and stars gliding across the ballroom walls. She imagined how lovely all the ladies in their dresses would look later that evening, spinning in circles along with the music.

Then suddenly the doors of the ballroom burst open and the King entered. He looked enraged. Snow had never seen him the least bit angry, and now this.

"Snow! What is the meaning of this?" he spat.

"Momma said I could see the ballroom before the feast..." Snow said, her sad eyes pleading with her father for understanding.

His anger did not subside.

"I would have never suspected you of such cruelty, Snow!"

Then, peeking from the large arched doorway, Snow saw them, Lucinda, Martha and Ruby, their dresses covered in mud, tattered and torn, their hair a frightful mess with little bits of twigs and leaves. There were bright patches of pink skin showing where the white paint had been scraped off their faces, sometimes through to the flesh. And Martha had lost one of her shiny black boots, revealing a green-and-silver striped stocking that had a large hole in the big toe, which she was desperately trying to hide with her other foot.

"I can't believe you would do such a thing!" said the King.

Martha was choking with deep sobs as she spoke. "She's a horrible, wicked girl—"

"Tricking us into falling into that hole!" Lucinda continued. "She planned it all along, I know—"

"She did, she hates us!" added Ruby, who was trying in vain to pull the twigs from her ringlets.

"Look at what the child did to us! She must be punished!" the odd sisters chimed in unison.

The King looked from his daughter to his cousins and said, "Indeed she shall!" and grabbed his daughter by the arm. "You will go to your chamber and not reappear until I have called for you, do you understand?"

The look on Snow's face was pure terror. She tried to protest, but the King would not allow for explanations. "Do not argue with me, Snow! I won't have my daughter acting so wretchedly. You are a *princess...*"

Just then, the Queen stepped in, enraged, and all but pounced upon her husband.

"What in the gods' names are you doing?" she

cried. "Take your hands off her! Take them *off*!"

The King looked shocked. "Excuse me?" he asked.

"Perhaps the battlefield and the cannon blasts have made you hard of hearing. Unhand her. And then explain to me why you are treating your daughter, *our* daughter, in this manner!"

Then the Queen noticed the sisters. She glared in their direction, and they shrunk back, attempting to slink away before the Queen could turn her anger upon them.

"As for you ladies," the Queen barked, "you will leave this court at *once*! I will have your belongings packed for you and sent along in another carriage as soon as it is convenient. I will *not* have you within these walls one more moment!"

Lucinda's voice was shrill as ever. "This is an outrage! We are the King's cousins, and we will not be—"

The Queen didn't give her, or either of the other two who might have finished her thought, an opportunity to do so.

"Guards, take these women directly to the

carriage outside. You are to ride with them in order to ensure they arrive home without mishap. Should they get up to any chicanery whatsoever, I will count upon you to put an end to it.

"Now, ladies, I suggest you vacate these premises before my husband hears what you've been up to. Cousins or not, you might find he will have less mercy in his heart than I have shown you this evening. Now leave my sight before I think the better of it and have you tossed into the dungeon to rot where you belong."

The King saw something in his wife he had never seen before, and it seemed to both impress and terrify him. As the guards took the sisters into shackles, Ruby muttered, "Is this absolutely—"

"Necessary? Perhaps there is another way out of this—" Lucinda continued.

"Room? We don't wish to be paraded through the great hall," Martha finished.

The Queen smiled at the sisters wickedly and said, "There *is* another way out as a matter of fact…" The sisters look relieved. The Queen continued,

"However, I think I'd much rather have everyone see you for the vile, disgraceful women you are."

The sisters looked defeated and hung their heads low as they were ushered away by the guards. As the sisters were taken away, they were met with reproachful looks from the other guests. Ladies whispered behind their gloved hands as they saw the sisters taken through the hall. Ruby all but fainted, completely overcome with shame, while Lucinda looked resolute with her chin held high as if she weren't completely besmirched in the eyes of the entire kingdom. The King appeared completely confounded as the Queen's manner did not seem to change when she addressed him after the odd sisters were removed.

"Kiss your daughter and tell her how much you love her," the Queen commanded.

The King blinked. He was the King. His word was law. But there was something in his wife's stern voice; there was a way about her that forced him to obey.

"I don't have time to explain this to you, husband.

You must trust I have done what is right; we will discuss it at some later time."

"Of course, my darling," the King said, all but bowing in supplication to his wife.

"Now tell her you're sorry for treating her so poorly, and let us go into the great hall and greet our guests."

The King again obeyed, and the Queen spun round, whipping up her cape like a whirling dervish as she stormed from the room and rejoined her uneasy guests at the celebration.

CHAPTER VIII

THE MAN IN THE MIRROR

It was nearly daybreak on the solstice before all the guests had departed and the King and Queen were able to retreat to their chamber. The Queen, whose countenance had not softened during the evening, directed her anger at her husband once more.

"I can't imagine what those witches told you to cause you to treat Snow so horribly."

The King hung his head.

"I've talked to Snow and assured her of my love for her. I told her I was deeply sorry and she has forgiven me, why can *you* not do the same?" he said.

The Queen's eyes filled with tears.

"My darling, what is it? Please tell me," the King pleaded.

The Queen looked directly into the King's eyes. "I never thought I would see you lay a hand on our daughter."

The King looked completely diminished.

"I didn't hurt her, my love, I swear to you."

"You hurt her *heart*," the Queen said, breaking down completely. "I know that look, that pained broken-hearted little face. It is the same one, the same face, I would stare at over and over again in my father's mirrors as a child. Oh, he was a cruel man. A real beast. To think my mother, my lovely, beautiful mother, was married to him. He hated me. Oh yes, he did, and he told me as much. 'Ugly, useless, senseless girl,' he would say. The words wounded deeper than the bruises and the scars from any physical pain he inflicted on me. At least those wounds healed."

The Queen collapsed to the floor, sitting there in the paradise of the castle with her face buried in her hands.

She looked up at the King, who gazed down upon her pitifully.

"Please, forgive me, dear," said the King. "You mentioned the battlefield earlier. You were correct, it does change you. It turns you into something more than a man... and at the same time something less. I was not myself."

The Queen saw this was true. She saw it in his eyes, and written on the scars on his face, and in the wildness of his unkempt hair.

"I will go check on Snow," the King said, clearly processing everything he had just learned of the Queen's early life.

"Of course, my darling, kiss her for me. I'm going to change for bed."

The King kissed the Queen, leaving her sitting on the edge of the massive four-poster bed. He kissed her again and went off to lay eyes on his sleeping girl, no doubt with the hope of easing his guilt-ridden conscience.

The Queen was utterly spent. She lay back on the feather bed, without the energy to change into her nightclothes. She heaved a deep sigh, rubbing her temples.

"Good evening, my Queen."

She sat bolt upright, expecting one of the guards with news of the sisters. But no one had entered the room, at least it didn't seem so.

"Over here, my Queen."

She directed her gaze to the opposite end of the room, where the voice seemed to be coming from.

"Hello? Is someone there?"

"Yes, my Queen."

"Show yourself then. And state your business, man."

She approached the hearth.

"Up above you, my Queen. There is no need to fear, my Queen."

The Queen looked above her, all around the chamber, even within the fiery hearth, but she could not see anyone.

"I am your slave," the voice said.

"My slave? This kingdom keeps no slaves."

"It is my duty to deliver you news of the

kingdom, anything you wish to know; I see far, I can show you anything you desire."

"Can you?"

"I see all, my Queen, into the hearts and minds of every last soul in the kingdom."

"Tell me then, where is the King?"

"With his daughter."

"You just heard him say as much before he left the room. What is happening now?"

"He is crying. He is deeply shamed by his treatment of the girl and how profoundly it hurt you."

The Queen felt dizzy.

"What is this lame trickery? You must have been in the room the whole while. Heard everything the King was saying. Now show yourself!"

"Please don't be frightened, my Queen, I'm here to assist you in all things. I am not the man you perceive me to be in your dreams, I cannot hurt you."

"You know of my dreams?"

"Indeed, my Queen. And though you have

been looking all about the room, you have not looked in the one place where you know you can find me."

The Queen's heart seemed to stop and all the blood in her body felt as if it were rushing to her head. She whipped round and tore the curtain from her father's mirror. Though she already half expected what she would find there, she was not prepared for the shock of seeing a living, moving face, hovering before her in the mirror. Her eyes grew wide with terror, her mouth gaped. It was a petrifying apparition, a disembodied head that looked like some sort of grotesque mask. Plumes of mystical smoke whirled around its hollow eyes and its long drooping mouth; its macabre face seemed forlorn.

"Who are you?" the Queen gasped.

"Do you not recognise me? Dear, has it been so long? Have the years that separated us caused you to forget me... enchantress?"

And in that moment, the Queen's face blanched. She recognised the face in the mirror, then promptly lost all ability to steady herself and collapsed.

But before she had fallen into blackness, she heard two final words ushered from the mouth of the visage in the mirror: "My daughter…"

CHAPTER IX

THE MAKER
OF MIRRORS

Hearing the crash, the King rushed to the Queen's chamber. He found the Queen awake but shaken, lying on the cold stone floor. The Queen was trembling, clutching the curtain she had torn from the mirror.

She looked up, but the man in the mirror was no longer there.

The King reached out to her, but she recoiled in horror.

"What is it, woman? Speak to me!"

"I'm, so sorry… my love… I didn't mean to… frighten you," the Queen said groggily, attempting to catch her breath. "I just... I must have fainted."

The Queen was dizzy. She couldn't find her own voice to further explain what had just happened, all she could manage was, "The mirror..."

The King looked to the mantel.

"Your father's mirror. Of course. This is why you have had such an aversion to it. Had I known everything you just told me, I never would have brought it into our home."

The Queen struggled to speak again. "Break it, please," she managed to mutter.

Without hesitation the King tore the mirror from the wall and smashed it into the mantel. Shattered glass littered the chamber floor like stardust sprinkled over a moonless sky.

The Queen sighed, relieved, though not entirely convinced that the mirror was destroyed for good. She gathered all her strength to speak.

"Before the day I met you, my lord, I dreaded visiting my father in his workshop. Seeing my face reflected back at me again and again only reminded me of how unsightly I was. A fact of which I didn't need reminding. A day of my childhood didn't pass when my father didn't tell me how unattractive I was, how ugly, and that is how I saw myself.

"My mother was beautiful; I knew that from the portrait that hung in my father's dingy little house. The one source of beauty in my life was that portrait, and I would stare at it for hours wondering why I wasn't beautiful like her. I didn't understand why my father was content to live in a rundown hovel of a house, when he could afford to live anywhere he desired. No matter how much I scrubbed, I couldn't rid the house of its stale, musty scent. I couldn't imagine my mother, so beautiful, living in that house, and I fancied that somehow the house, too, must have been mourning my mother's death. I fancied that while she was alive it was probably a pleasant little cottage where birds would alight to feed on the windowsills, and flowers bloomed all around. But after her death, everything within the house was mouldering and distressed, all except for my mother's things, which my father kept locked away. Sometimes I would go through her trunks and adorn myself with her old dresses and jewellery. Lovely dresses with intricate beadwork and jewels that sparkled like the stars. She seemed to love beautiful, delicate things, and I wondered if she had lived, would she have loved me, too, ugly as I was?

"Stories of my father's love for my mother were known throughout the lands. Tales of the maker of mirrors and his beautiful wife were told throughout every kingdom like an ancient myth woven with strands of love and sorrow. My father made beautiful mirrors of all shapes and sizes, lovely mirrors that inspired the great kings and queens to travel over hill and dale just to purchase one of his gorgeous and enchanting treasures.

"My mother loved the winter solstice, and my father would make the grandest spectacle of the occasion. He made tiny mirrors in the shapes of suns, moons and stars and hung them in all the trees on their grounds. Candles, too, decorated the trees, casting the most magnificent light reflected in the mirrors, so that their home could be seen for miles around; a tiny magical city illuminated and glowing in a sea of wintry darkness. He was heard to remark upon the gorgeous glow he created around his home every winter, saying it was pale in comparison to the beauty of his wife: her raven hair, fair skin and sparkling onyx eyes, the sort that tilt up at the corners, adding a catlike quality to them. How I wished someone would love me the way my father loved his wife; so inspired by her beauty, he created intricate treasures so she could see her grace reflected back at her. I thought I would never know that love, or know what it was to be beautiful. And then I met you in my father's mirror shop.

"When you ventured off promising to return, leaving me alone and bewildered, my father's reaction sent my heart racing into panic. 'Clearly you have bewitched him, daughter. Soon enough he will see you for the vile hag you are,' he told me. I attempted to convince him I was no witch. I knew no enchantments. But he persisted. 'Do not think a man such as he would have you as a wife. You are too old, daughter, and unsightly; you are unremarkable in every way.'

"My mother's death was a result of my birth, and I am sure my father blamed me for it, seeing my resemblance to her as a taunting insult added to the injury of his loss. My father never talked about the night my mother died, but I heard tiny shards of the story and pieced them together in my imagination, like reflections in one of his broken mirrors.

"I imagined my mother writhing in terrible agony. In my mind I saw her clutching her bulging stomach in pain, crying out to her husband for help as the midwife tended to her. My father helpless, his face white and ghastly, filled with fear as my mother lay there lifeless after giving birth, and his eyes filled with revulsion when he looked upon the little creature that ripped his dearest love from his life. My father must have hated me from that day. Whenever he looked upon my face, it was with disgust.

"Once, I must have been five or six years of age, I was standing in our yard, the sun streaming through the canopy of trees. I was holding a bunch of wildflowers when my father came upon me. 'What are you doing with those flowers, girl?' he asked; his face was screwed up in controlled anger. I told him that I wanted to bring the flowers to my mother. He stared at me blankly and cruelly. 'You didn't even know her! Why would she want flowers from you?' I remember being too sad, too shocked to cry as I responded, 'She was my momma, and I love her.'

"He just looked at me in that way I had become accustomed to. That way that told me if I said anything more he would strike me. Sometimes he would strike me even if I remained silent. That day, I just stood there and held out the flowers, looking up at him with my lip quivering, my eyes on the verge of tears, but too overcome with so many different emotions to express them by crying outright. He tore the flowers from my tiny hand. Then he turned his back on me and walked out of the courtyard. I hoped that he would place the flowers on my mother's grave, but I am all but certain he never did.

"I promised myself I wouldn't let my father's demons taint my soul. I swore that I was starting a new life with you. I wanted to forget him and be happy with you and my beautiful little bird. I vowed I would make Snow my own daughter and love her the way I wished my father had loved me. That I would tell Snow White how beautiful she was every day of her life, and we would dance together and laugh. And unlike my father, I would take Snow to visit her mother's grave and use the letters you entrusted me with to tell her what her mother was like.

"I resolved to never think of the maker of mirrors ever again. He belongs to the darkness now. The day my father died it was as if my life was set ablaze, as if his descent into darkness brought me into a shining world where I was finally able to find love and happiness. That very hour, I brought every one of his mirrors outside our home and hung them from a giant tree on the grounds. It was the most remarkable spectacle I'd ever seen, the mirrors swaying in the breeze, catching the sunlight and reflecting it in the most magnificent way. The sight of it took my breath away. The townsfolk thought it was beautiful too. They believed it was a tribute to my father, and I let them believe that. They needn't know what a horrible man he was, they needn't know I was for the first time coming out into the light, that I was no longer lingering in darkness and in doubt. *That* was the true reason I had celebrated.

"No one knew how much he hated me, how cruel and utterly inhuman his soul was. A soul, ha! I wonder if he ever had one. He must have at some point. His love for my mother was so great. Perhaps his soul died with her the night she left this world.

"Still, whatever was left of him was pure evil. I had sat by his deathbed, caring for him, trying to keep him alive because, in my heart of hearts, I knew that it was right, to treat the blood of your blood that way. Still, he had nothing but hatred and bitter words for me, 'He will never come for you, you know. You've always been an ugly child. What would a *king* want with the likes of you?' I was there as he left this world. Right by his side. Holding on to his hand so that he would not need to journey into that great unknown alone. And the moment before he died, his near-lifeless eyes looked up at me. I was full of folly, ready to believe that he was going to thank me. Instead he said, 'I have never loved you, daughter.' And then he closed his eyes and left this world."

The King sat silently. He rested his chin on his folded hands as he rocked back and forth, contemplating all he had just learned. Then he knelt down next to the Queen and took her into his arms.

"I wish he were alive today," the King said, "so I could slay him with my own hands for all he has done."

The Queen looked up at her husband, who she had known only to be filled with love. To love even his enemies. Did he truly care for her so much that he would even betray his own beliefs?

This was the man she loved above all others. She touched his hand, callous with battle scars and the weight of artillery and wielding of swords. She locked her hands in his, crawled into his arms, then kissed him lightly on the lips. His once-soft mouth was now chapped and chafed from exposure to the elements. He tasted like sweat and, the Queen thought, blood.

Why, she wondered, must things change? Why could she not have frozen time the day she was married, lived happily ever after with Snow and the King? Why could she not create peace on earth so that her husband would not ever need to leave her again?

She wondered this very thing for the next month, while she still had the King with her. But on the twenty-third day of January, the King left again.

"Papa, I'm going to miss you," said Snow.

"I promise to come home to you soon, my Snow. I always do, don't I?"

The little girl nodded.

"I love you, and I will miss you, dear," the King said with a deep sigh.

"I love you too, Papa!"

The King kissed his daughter and spun her round, which made her giggle. "I will miss you both with all my heart. You'll both be with me."

The Queen and Snow stood in the courtyard and watched as the King and his men ventured over snow-covered mountains on horseback. Their torches glowed in the dark winter afternoon, and the air was the kind of cold that glassed your eyes over; a type of cold you can practically see. The King's army grew smaller and smaller, like ants climbing piles of sugar.

Then they dipped below the horizon and the King was gone.

CHAPTER X

THE SHATTERING OF A SOUL

To the Queen the days felt like months and the weeks like years while the King was away. The castle was so quiet. She missed the days when it was filled with Snow's joyful laughter as she was chased by her growling father, who was pretending to be a dragon or a warlock.

Soon, she told herself, soon he will return and with him life will once again fill the stone walls of the castle.

But for now, the castle might as well have been lifeless. The Queen sat in a comfortable throne alongside the fireplace in her chamber, lost in one of her favourite manuscripts, the *Song of Roland*. But everything about it reminded her of the King, and so she set it aside and called upon her servants to draw a bath for her.

Far more quickly than she had anticipated, a rap was upon her door.

"Your Highness, Your Majesty..." said the timid, quivering young girl in the doorway. The Queen had not seen her before and realised she must have been a new servant.

"Calm down, dear, I am a Queen, not a witch," the Queen said, smiling.

"Yes, well, this here," the girl held out a large, wrapped package that was nearly as tall as she was, "this arrived for you here today. The guards have examined it, and it appears to pose no... no danger..."

The girl put the package down and stared at the Queen, who looked at the package sceptically.

"From whence does it come?" the Queen asked.

"It arrived with this note," the girl said, holding out a rolled parchment, which twitched like a windblown leaf in the girl's shaking hand. "I am not... not privy to what it says herein, and so I am not aware of its... its origins."

The Queen quickly grabbed the parchment and unrolled it.

The parchment was much larger than necessary, and contained the note:

FOR YOUR HOSPITALITY

The Queen raised an eyebrow.

"You say you do not know what it contains?" the Queen asked.

"I do not, Your... Your Majesty," the girl said quietly, "but the guards have confirmed that it is harmless," she reminded the Queen.

The Queen paused for a moment, then continued, "Very well, then, bring it in."

The girl struggled with the large package, which was wrapped unevenly in ragged linens, making it impossible to determine the actual shape or size of whatever was inside. A few men rushed over to assist her, and it took four of them to get the package into the Queen's chamber.

"Will there be anything more, my... my Queen?" the girl asked.

The Queen shook her head, and the girl curtsied and quickly left the room, followed by the men.

The Queen paced before the package. It could have been from any one of the guests who attended the solstice celebration. A token of gratitude and good will. The guards had checked it, after all.

So why was she so hesitant to open it?

The Queen stared at the awkwardly wrapped gift. She reread the parchment. Then she steeled herself and tore the linens open at their seams.

"Good morning, my Queen," the face in the mirror said, staring out at her from behind a cloak of frayed linen.

It smiled an evil, cunning grin.

The Queen screamed and recoiled from the mirror.

"You have been lonely," the Slave said.

"What is it to you, demon?" the Queen responded.

"You have been thinking of your husband, wanting his company. But I am all you need, my Queen," the Slave said.

"What could you offer me, evil one?" the Queen snapped.

"As I told you, I see all in the kingdom. I could tell you what your daughter's favourite memories are, or your sister, Verona, I could reveal her deepest secrets to you. But it is your *husband* you have been thinking of mainly these days, is it not? I could tell you where he is, what he is doing. Let me do so... Ah, yes, the most recently I can see him is a few days prior to this. Hmm... I wonder why that is so? He is aboard his steed. His sword is raised high in the air. Oh! An arrow has nearly hit his cheek. He looks to be grazed. Yes, there is blood, a great deal of it, dripping from his jawbone. And a great deal of noise. But he is proud and brave. A true warrior. He is bleeding, but he will continue to fight. He will be safe. They make quite a ruckus out there on the battlefield, do they not? Oh, now, what is this? A man with a lance, coming up right behind him. I say, I do not think your husband sees his attacker. If only we could warn him. If only we could somehow prevent the spear from entering his back and impaling him straight through so the weapon emerges from his chest... to prevent him from..."

"Fiend!" the Queen screamed. "Stop this at once! You speak these lies as if they are the immortal truth!"

The Slave smiled slightly and knowingly, then fixed his stare upon the Queen.

"No!" she cried, grabbing a nearby glass jar for oils and ointments and shattering it against the mirror. "Lies!" the Queen cried.

Verona rushed into her room. Her eyes were bloodshot and her face was streaked with tears. "My Queen," Verona said through a quavering voice. Then she flung her arms around the Queen and rocked on the floor with her. "You've heard the news then? The terrible, awful news?"

The Queen looked up into Verona's tearful eyes.

Verona continued, "His body is in transport now."

The Queen covered her mouth with her shaking hand, her eyes wide, staring at Verona in disbelief.

He couldn't possibly be dead; she had just seen him a few short months ago. He was just injured; yes, injured and on his way back to mend his wounds. The Slave in the mirror was a liar! And the messages from the field were never reliable. Someone always got something wrong. He was hurt, but it was nothing serious. And he was returning to her. Here. Home. Now.

"No, he's coming home! He's coming home," was all the Queen could say.

Verona shook her head. The Queen's face, hair and clothes were soaked with tears that belonged to both her and Verona. The pain in her chest tightened its grip as she slowly absorbed the reality of her husband's death.

Gone!

She would never see him again, never hear his bright laugh, never again sit by the fire and watch him play dragons with Snow or tell her stories of the witches who lived in the forest.

"You may leave," the Queen said to Verona with as much composure as she could gather.

Verona put her hands on the Queen's shoulders.

"Please let me stay with you."

"No, Verona, I need some time to myself."

The moment Verona left the room the Queen felt the great weight of grief and anger. She could not breathe. Surely she wouldn't survive this pain. One cannot hurt so profoundly and live on, she thought; it was unfathomable to spend the rest of her days in such agony, without her dearest love by her side.

It was better to die.

But then what of Snow White?

And how could she even face the child? Tell her such horrible news? It would crush her, clearly break her heart. The Queen stood up on weak knees, and, clutching the walls and railings, she made her way slowly down the stairs, which seemed to sway beneath her.

Out in the courtyard, Snow was sitting at the well. The Queen felt an unusually sharp pang upon seeing her now. Snow watched a little bluebird eat bread crumbs upon the well's wall. She looked transfixed and in her own world, a world in which her father was away, but still alive.

The Queen was acutely aware that she would be changing this child's life forever, shattering her world with a few words: *your father is dead.*

She played it in her mind as she approached the girl. Her daughter. She would now be all that Snow had in the world.

When she finally reached the child, she couldn't bring herself to say it out loud; if she did it would make it real, and she couldn't face such a harsh reality. She wanted to be strong for Snow, but uttering such gut-wrenching words would cause her to break down completely.

So, she buried her grief deep within her. She choked on the words as she forced them from her throat.

"Snow, my sweet girl, my little bird, I have to tell you something."

Snow looked up from the bluebird she was feeding and smiled at her mother. "Hello, Momma!" Snow said, smiling brightly.

The Queen struggled to remain composed as she took a seat next to the girl on the edge of the well. Snow White's face brightened.

"Is it Papa? Is he coming home today? Can we have a party just like we did at the start of winter?"

"Little bird..." the Queen's voice broke and trailed off.

"Momma, what's wrong?"

The Queen shook her head, and closed her eyes tight to dam the tears.

Snow looked at her mother with sad, black eyes and said, "He's not coming back yet, is he? Not now?"

The Queen shook her head. "Not ever."

"I think maybe you're wrong, Momma, he promised he would come home soon, and Papa never breaks his promises."

The Queen's grief intensified. She choked it down and felt it grip at her, slicing at her insides like pieces of glass. She felt broken, no longer able to contain her tears.

"I know, my poppet, but I'm not mistaken. He couldn't help it, my darling, he isn't coming home this time."

The little girl's lip quivered and she began to shake. The Queen held out her arms to her, and Snow White crumpled into her mother's lap and howled an unearthly sob. The child was shaking so violently that the Queen felt she might crush the little girl for holding her too tightly. As she hugged Snow she wished to take the child's grief and lock it away inside her with her own.

She was hopeless and helpless.

As she led Snow back to the castle she realised she was walking into another world altogether, a world that would be forever altered. She couldn't imagine it. She felt lost, floating in a nightmare, numb and inhuman. She looked at herself in a mirror that hung in the grand hall, simply to remind herself she was still *in* the world. All of this felt as if it couldn't be happening. And yet, it was.

Verona appeared at the end of the hall, distraught.

"Verona, please come collect Snow," the Queen said.

"No! Momma! Don't leave me!" Snow cried.

Verona came to the Queen's side to gather the girl. But Snow clung tightly to the Queen's legs.

"No! Momma! Don't leave me! I'm scared," she screamed as Verona pried her off her mother.

The Queen remained steely and cold and made her way to her chamber, where she soon collapsed under the terrible sneering gaze of the Slave in the mirror.

CHAPTER XI

FAREWELLS

As the days went on, the Queen would feel the King's hand in hers as she slept. She sometimes heard his steps upon the stairs, or his rapping at her chamber door. Occasionally, she heard a laugh that she thought belonged to him. In these moments, she told herself that it had all been a terrible mistake and that he was home, alive, with her. But those moments quickly faded as the hazy cloud of despair dissipated and reality forced itself upon her.

She would make promises to the gods vowing to be a better wife if she could have her husband back. She felt wicked for shaming him at the winter solstice festival. She wanted to tell him how much she loved him. He had to have known. She couldn't stand the thought of him not knowing.

When the time came, she could not look upon his body. Instead, she asked Verona to do the deed for her. And she put off making the funerary arrangements for as long as she could. Days, or possibly weeks, had passed since his death and the Queen was bombarded with requests for details about the funeral. They seemed to come by the quarter-hour from all the lands, piles of them brought in on silver trays by women with swollen eyes, the entire household grieving, the castle haunted by attendants wearing black armbands, puffy white faces and quiet dispositions.

Everyone tiptoed around the Queen as if she might break at any moment. Perhaps some of them wondered how she hadn't done so already.

And all this time, the Slave in the mirror did not show his face. Strangely, she had begun to desire his presence. If he could see all in the kingdom, then why not beyond it? And beyond *that* to the great unknown? But now that she longed for his image to appear, he was nowhere to be seen.

Her longing, her agony, was so great, but only Verona saw her cry. The Queen would lock herself in the morning room looking out past the garden towards the courtyard and the well, just looking at the flowers stirring in the breeze, remembering her wedding day. A servant would bring a plate of sandwiches and tea, removing the untouched dishes only a short time later.

Sometimes she would think she saw the King walking his customary path back home to her. She would imagine herself running up to greet him, kissing his face as he lifted her into the air like a little girl. The piles of letters that continued to accumulate sat unopened in front of her.

"My poor girl."

An older woman with bright silver hair pulled into two large buns on either side of her head was standing on the threshold of the morning room. Her hair glistened in the sunlight, her eyes twinkled with tears and kindness. Who was this woman? An angel, coming to claim the Queen?

Then a familiar face stepped up behind the woman. It was Uncle Marcus. The woman must have been Aunt Vivian.

The Queen stood to greet them, and Marcus pulled her close and embraced her. He felt warm and real; she felt safe and protected in his arms. Her heart threatened to break under the weight of his kindness.

"Hello, Uncle, I'm so happy to see you," she said flatly, as if she could hardly believe she'd ever feel anything close to happiness ever again.

"We're here now, dear. Me, and your Aunt Viv, we're here to help you."

"You name it, dear and I will do it," said Vivian. "*Anything*, my dear, if there is anything I can do, please let me know. I've been where you are, dear. Sick for months. Couldn't get out of bed. Oh, I know all the tricks. We'll have you back up and running as soon as possible. You mark my word, darling."

The Queen nodded absently.

"Why don't I start by opening these letters for

you? No sense in you having to go through these now. No sense at all. I'll take them all if you don't mind."

The Queen suddenly felt embarrassed. "I'm sorry, I didn't ring for refreshments or have someone show you to your rooms," she said, her eyes glassy with grief.

"That's all been taken care of, dear. Verona saw to it. Don't you worry about us dear, we're here to help you. Now, what can I get *you*? Perhaps some hot tea; that pot looks cold. And I think we should get some food in you. You look as if you've not eaten properly in weeks," Aunt Viv said.

The Queen shook her head.

"Don't bother going against her, Majesty," Marcus said. "She will have you stuffed before you can say no. Acquiesce. I learned a long time ago it is much easier. And tastier, too." Marcus patted his paunchy belly.

The Queen smiled for the first time since she'd lost her husband. It was a weak, almost forced smile, but a smile nonetheless. It was nice to have someone older to count upon. Someone who had been so close to her husband.

With Aunt Viv's help, funeral arrangements were finally made. The King's body was taken to the mausoleum on a rainy morning. It was carried in an ornate horse-drawn carriage that had brought the King's father and all his father's forbears before him to their graves. Ahead of the carriage were two large shiny black horses, who seemed to be mourning the King's loss along with the rest of the kingdom.

Inside the carriage, the King's coffin was covered with flowers. Red roses. The Queen's favourite. He had requested it in the papers he had left before his first campaign away from her. The Queen wore a black dress with deep red beading. Her hair was pulled into a lavish braid and coiled upon her head. She was shielded from the rain by servants who held a thick black cloth over her head. Snow, the broken child, was outfitted in a dress of the deepest red. The Queen wondered if the girl would ever be happy again. And, if so, would she have the right to be?

The Queen, who had not appeared publicly since the King's death, stood, with Verona's help, as the body was stowed away in the mausoleum. Verona put her arm around her Queen, her friend, and led her and Snow back to the carriage, to be transported back to the castle.

"'Tis a pity—"

"Such a shame, really—"

"So young, so—"

"Beautiful, he was, and now... gone."

The Queen looked up.

The sisters.

"We needed to be here," Lucinda said.

"We hope you don't mind," Martha continued.

"After all, we parted on such sour terms, last visit," Ruby finished.

The Queen was too exhausted from grief to feel anything but apathy towards the sisters. Now was not the time to become incensed.

"Thank you," the Queen replied.

"We assume—" Lucinda continued.

"You have received our gift?" Martha finished.

The Queen nodded absently, not even truly processing which gift they were speaking of. Not thinking about the mirror at all.

"He can be a bit cold-hearted and brutish, that father of yours," Ruby said. "Please do let us know if he needs taming."

Verona glared at the sisters standing there, soaked from the rain. She was tired of their cryptic talk and riddles. She jerked the Queen and her daughter closer to her side, ushering them away from the sisters and into their carriage. The sisters took quick, short, birdlike steps away from the funeral, and the Queen wasn't sure if it was her grief playing tricks on her or if she really did hear laughter coming from the sisters as they went away.

CHAPTER XII

THE QUEEN
IN SOLITUDE

The Queen had taken to her bed for many weeks after the funeral. She felt conflicted about refusing Snow when she came to visit. She wanted so desperately to comfort the girl, but she could not. Seeing the child only reminded her of her husband. His eyes seemed to look at her from Snow's face. And similarly, seeing the Queen in this state would surely disturb the poor girl.

But it wasn't only Snow. Since the King's death, the Queen had refused all visitors, save one. Verona had been ever at the Queen's side, pleading with her to get out of doors and into the sunshine.

"My Queen, won't you see your daughter today?" Verona pleaded. "Perhaps you can take a walk about the grounds. She misses you terribly. It's been weeks since you've emerged. She loves Uncle Marcus, Aunt Viv and the Huntsman, but she needs you."

"I'm not up to it just yet, Verona," the Queen responded.

"Very well. Remember me whenever you are in your darkest moments. I will be here for you whenever I am called upon."

"I know, sister. And I am grateful for it. Now please, let me be."

Verona curtsied and left the room, but the Queen knew she had every intention of returning. Verona had not been able to spend much time away from the Queen.

As soon as she was certain the door had locked, the Queen walked over to the mirror, a ritual she engaged in daily since the funeral. She longed for the Slave to appear there. She wanted, needed, news of her husband and assurance of his well-being in the world beyond.

But all that stared back at her when she searched there was her own reflection.

She stared at herself, broken and numb. She looked ragged and haggard. Her swollen eyes and puffy cheeks accentuated her blemishes and other imperfections. And her hair had been neither washed nor braided in weeks.

She despaired over what she'd become. Perhaps her former beauty was simply an enchantment after all... one cast by her husband. And when he died, her beauty, a *false* beauty, died with him. How could she have ever thought herself to be beautiful? That she looked like her gorgeous mother, or rivaled, in any way, the King's first wife, or even little Snow?

Then, as she stared at her hated face in the mirror, on the brink of a despair she would never be able to recover from, something began to take shape beyond the glass. In a swirling mist inside the mirror, the Slave appeared. The Queen felt a twinge of hope and possibly even joy, leap up inside of her.

"It has been quite some time, daughter. Did

you enjoy the funeral?" the Slave asked.

The Queen's lip stiffened. "It was a beautiful ceremony befitting a beautiful man and celebrating his life. And now I need something from you."

"And what is that?"

"News of my husband."

The face in the mirror laughed. "News of the King ended with his life."

"Can you not see all?" the Queen asked.

"I cannot see beyond the grave. But I have the ability to see all things in these lands. I can see things that can make you terribly sad. And I can see things that might even make you very, very happy."

"What could possibly make me happy again now that my husband is dead?" the Queen asked.

"I think you know," the face replied, and then faded from view.

The Queen banged on the glass and called out to the Slave, but he was gone. Though the Queen did not know when he would return, she suspected he would. When he did, she would be prepared.

And in the meantime, she had a message to send.

Though they lived almost an entire land away, the sisters arrived just a day after the Queen sent for them. Verona sneered and scowled as they made their way into the castle scuttling about, chattering, as usual. She viewed the speed of their arrival as one more odd happening to add to the list of those the sisters had accumulated. Snow White made herself scarce, and the attendants at the court all seemed reasonably disturbed by the women.

They did not have to deal with them for long, however. The Queen requested that the sisters be brought to her chamber immediately upon their arrival at the court.

"Sisters," the Queen said, "welcome."

"We are—" Lucinda said.

"Privileged," Ruby finished.

"The scars of your husband's loss show upon you," Martha said, reaching out and plucking a grey hair from the Queen's head.

The Queen shifted uncomfortably. At one time she would have banished the sisters from the kingdom forever for doing such a thing. But there was something she needed, and she knew only the sisters could deliver it.

"Last we met..." the Queen began.

"The funeral, such a sad day, yes, sad, sad, very sad," the sisters clucked.

"Last we met," the Queen began again, ignoring their interruptions, "you spoke of my mirror."

Three eerie smiles spread across the sisters' faces in tandem.

"The Magic Mirror," Lucinda said.

"The portal to the Other World," Ruby continued.

"The one which contains the soul of the maker of mirrors," Martha said.

"So you know of it," the Queen acknowledged.

"Of course we do! It was—"

"We who created it—"

"Though not created it, as in tempered and gilded—"

"But we who captured the Mirror Maker's soul—"

"Not captured"—Lucinda spat—"he granted it to us—"

"And we captured it, tied it up in spider silk webbing, as it floated out of his body and up, up, up—"

"And we who took it and locked it away—"

"In the Magic Mirror. Don't forget, sisters—"

"It was he who had asked, he who had begged—"

"He who bartered his soul away."

The sisters began to cackle again.

The Queen stared at the women coolly. "I demand you tell more. What is this barter you speak of?"

The sisters began a tale that was less fragmented than the Queen had ever heard usher from their lips.

They spoke as one. "You see, the maker of mirrors, his wife wanted a child, wanted a child more than anything. Yet she was barren. And the maker of mirrors could not bear to see her unhappy. And we, we cannot bear to see one so unhappy, so we engaged the maker of mirrors. We told him, that for a price, we could make it so that his wife might bear fruit. But the cost was not small—"

"His soul," the Queen finished.

The sisters nodded in agreement, then continued.

"So, the child was hers and his, but he owed us dearly..."

The Queen was perplexed by her emotions. She should hate the sisters for what they had done to her father, but the Queen herself so hated the man that she took great comfort in the sisters' weird imprisonment of him.

"Go on," the Queen commanded.

"So when the child was born, we sealed the deal for his soul, and he had his gift, his child. We would claim his soul once he shuffled off this mortal coil. A pity, an irony, that your mother would not live to appreciate his sacrifice."

"We delivered the mirror to your husband," Lucinda said.

"And did you the favour of having him give it to you," Ruby finished.

"Oh dear, how hard it must have been for you to be without either of your loving parents," Martha said, grinning.

"But now, with the Magic Mirror, your father is always near," Lucinda said, grinning now, too.

"I believe you said something to me at the funeral. About the mirror. About my father. About taming the spirit within," the Queen said, ill at ease with the conversation and becoming increasingly anxious.

"Are you experiencing problems? Is it not working quite right? Are you having some trouble calling upon your father, my dear?" the sisters asked, moving dizzyingly from one speaker to the next.

"Yes," the Queen said. "Can you show me how to tame the spirit?"

The sisters chuckled.

"Are you certain that is what you wish?" they asked.

The Queen nodded.

"You might find yourself ruined by the things—"

"He tells you."

"Go on. I command you," the Queen snapped.

The sisters shuffled over to the mirror and linked their hands. They held their arms over their heads and began to chant:

Slave in the Magic Mirror,
Come from the farthest space.
Through wind and darkness we summon thee.
Speak! Let us see thy face.

A cool wind began to blow through the room, and the curtains danced like ghosts. A flame appeared in the mirror, and then the face appeared in a swirling purple mist, just as it had all those times before. But something was different. The face in the mirror was almost expressionless and much more docile than it had previously been. Was what they said true? Had their incantation tamed him?

"What wouldst thou know, sisters?"

The sisters chuckled and sniggered.

"Why have you been so very unruly for your new mistress?" the sisters asked.

"I have not been kind to Her Majesty, this I know and this you can see, for she has never summoned me with the power that shackled me by thee."

The sisters laughed again. "You may leave now, Slave," the sisters said. And the face in the Magic Mirror dissolved in a swirling purple whirl.

"Does this tutorial suit Your Majesty?" the sisters asked.

"Very much so," the Queen said, smiling. "You may go now."

"Before you send us on our way—" Lucinda said.

"We've left you another gift—" Ruby continued.

"You will find it in your dungeon. Use it—" Martha said.

"Well," Ruby finished.

When evening fell and the sisters had left the court, the Queen approached the Magic Mirror, still tired, but more hopeful now that she would find what she looked for there. She was so fixed on the mirror that she did not give the sisters' second gift a thought. She gazed into the reflective glass and considered what she would ask. Then she recited the sisters' incantation and called forth the Slave in the mirror.

"What wouldst thou know, my Queen?" the Slave asked.

"I wish to know of my husband. Is he well? Is he among the gods or the demons?"

"I have told you before, my Queen, I cannot see beyond that which can be seen."

The Queen considered this. All hope that she would know what had been in store for her husband after his death swiftly left her. She could barely see her reflection beyond the face in the mirror. But what she could see terrified her. She was as ugly as her father had always said she was. There was only one thing other than news of her husband that might lift her spirits.

"Tell me, mirror, who it is that is fairest in the land?" she said desperately.

"Are you certain that you wish for me to answer that request?" the Slave asked.

"Certain," the Queen said gritting her teeth.

"Know that I am bound by the truth," the Slave replied.

"Then, if it is not I, tell me who it is," the Queen said, becoming enraged.

"I did not say it was not you. I told you I could not lie. I thought you should be aware before treading into this territory."

The Queen sneered and nodded.

"Who is she, Slave? Who is the fairest one of all?" the Queen asked.

"You have been weathered by this experience. You are worn and…" the Slave said.

"Out with it, man!" the Queen yelled, pounding her fist upon the mantel and shouting. "Who is fairest in all the land?"

"You are, my Queen," the Slave replied. Then he disappeared in a swirl of mist, and the Queen could once again see her face. Her eyes narrowed and a wicked grin stretched across one corner of her mouth.

CHAPTER XIII

ENVY

Shortly after her exchange with the Slave in the mirror, the Queen finally emerged from her chamber, looking as regal as ever. And it had been as Verona said it would be; the kingdom had waited to embrace the Queen as their sole ruler. And they did so in the grandest fashion imaginable.

The day was a whirlwind of red rose petals floating magically in the air, evoking the day she married the King, which caused a tight pain in her chest and the threat of tears. Snow rushed to the Queen and hugged her around her knees. Verona stood beside them and smiled.

"Oh Momma, I've missed you so much!" the girl cried. Uncle Marcus and Aunt Viv waved from the sidelines as the Queen took Snow in her arms and the gathered crowds cheered.

The day was filled with festivals, banquets and merriment. And as evening fell and the Queen retired to her room, she found herself armed with a new confidence. She approached the mirror in her chamber and said to her reflection, "I am the fairest of all."

She felt renewed, not just by the kingdom's embrace of her, but something else entirely. All those years ago, after her father's death, she had thought she had exorcised his ghost from her mind. But it wasn't so. Not until she watched his face tell her how beautiful she was, the fairest in the land, in fact, did she feel such a weight lifted. She had power over him now, the way he'd had it over her for so many years. And she was going to exercise it.

She called forth the Slave in the mirror, just as the sisters had taught her. When he appeared in lapping tongues of flame and plumes of purple smoke, she recited the sisters' incantation, then continued, "Magic Mirror on the wall, who is the fairest one of all?"

The Slave, who was bound by honesty, admitted to the Queen that she was the fairest of them all, and the Queen was put at ease. The fear that she had grown into the haggard witch her father once labelled her melted away. Any insecurities she might have had vanished. Even her deep sorrow over the loss of her king was allayed when she heard and saw the Slave in the mirror; the soul, the very *face*, of her father who once battered her with demeaning and disparaging words, admit that she was beautiful; that she was the fairest in the land.

The Queen soon found that on days when she had forgotten to consult the mirror, she was ornery, bitter and anxious. She snapped easily at her attendants, even those people closest to her: Verona and Snow. She would find herself short of breath, with a tightness in her chest. And she knew that the only way to cure these ills was to relent to her obsession and return to the mirror, to her father's face, to hear him say that she was lovely. That she was beautiful. That she was fairest of all.

And so, it became a ritual for the Queen. Each day she consulted the Magic Mirror, engulfed and possessed by her vanity, still bereft over the death of her husband. She used her father's validation to cure all her fevered nightmares of loss, of growing old, of being the thing, the terrible ugly woman, her father had always told her that she was.

The mirror, for its part, always told the Queen the truth. That she was the fairest in the kingdom. And then, unexpectedly, it gave the Queen a different answer.

"Famed is your beauty, Your Majesty, but another lovely maid I see…"

A terrible rage boiled within the Queen. She felt transformed. She had never experienced a feeling like this before. It felt terrible and absolutely wonderful all at once. She never knew such jealousy, or that such an emotion could stir up such anger, perhaps even hatred. And with that hatred, an undeniable *power*.

"Who? Who is it? Speak, Slave!" the Queen barked.

"Grief and loss, my Queen, have not diminished her beauty; her face is not lined with tragedy. Nor is she marred with pain and suffering as you have so clearly been. This maidservant—"

"Maidservant?" the Queen said sharply.

"I cannot deny that you are beautiful, my Queen. But I also cannot lie. You are outshined by Verona. She is the only woman within the kingdom who outstrips you in beauty."

"How I wished for your love when I was a girl, how I would have thrived if you had just shown me one little bit of approval! And now, you use it to destroy me and the woman I care for most in this land, the only family I have left? No, I do not believe you. In fact I do not believe that this is happening at all. I must be dreaming or under some spell, I am sure I will awake and find this was all a horrid dream conjured by my suffering and grief!" the Queen said.

"Would you be happier then without me, my Queen? It was your calling me that brought me here in the first place; but if my being here causes you pain, I will happily leave you, until you call upon me again," the Slave told her. And her father's image disappeared from the mirror.

Just then, Verona walked into the room, holding Snow by the hand and glowing with blissfulness. Verona was so fair and so lovely. And for the first time in her life, the Queen hated her for it.

"Apologies for disturbing you, Your Majesty," Verona said. "But the reception celebrating an entire moon since your return to us is about to begin, and we thought we would accompany you to the great hall where everyone is waiting to receive you."

"Yes, of course; thank you, Verona," the Queen said. But she suddenly felt none of the sisterly love she'd always had for Verona.

"Then shall we proceed?" Verona asked, clearly growing uncomfortable from the Queen's stares.

"Not until I've kissed my lovely daughter, Snow. And how are you on this day, my lovely little creature?"

"Happy to see you, Momma. I missed you while

you were sick and am so happy you've been well for so long."

"I missed you too, my little bird, I'm sorry I didn't see you as often as I should have while I was unwell."

"I'm happy to see you now, Momma. You look very pretty today, and so does Verona. Don't you think so, Momma?"

"Yes, she looks quite lovely," the Queen said flatly. "Very well then, let's proceed and enjoy this day the way it was intended."

And the three beauties made their way to the great hall. Could it have been the Queen's imagination, or were many eyes truly upon Verona as they arrived? The Queen attempted to banish all thoughts of what the Slave had said about Verona. But it was impossible to distract herself from his words. And as the evening and the following days passed, the Slave in the mirror always answered the same way.

Verona was the fairest of all.

The Queen felt torn between her love for this

woman who had been like a sister to her, and for her father. But was it *love* she felt for her father? No, it was something more terrible than love. His approval was an obsession and an addiction. And Verona, simply by being in the court, was preventing the Queen from receiving the daily affirmation from her father that she so needed.

And why would she want such approval from her father? What would it say about his nature that he would find her beautiful again simply for acting on jealousy? What would it say of *hers*?

So, the Queen told herself it wasn't for vanity's sake when she finally decided to send Verona away to a neighbouring kingdom on a diplomatic assignment. No, it was merely for the sake of the Queen's own peace of mind, and in the interest of preserving the women's friendship.

For Verona, the goodbye was tearful. Snow, too, could not contain her sorrow. After all, the child had lost so much. And now the woman who was closest to her after her stepmother was departing as well. The Queen remained stony, icy, unmoved.

And directly after Verona's carriage pulled away, the Queen whipped up her cape and returned to her chamber and the Magic Mirror.

The Queen slammed her door shut and stalked towards the mirror. She hesitated. What if it did not work? What if Verona was only the first of many in the kingdom who were fairer than she? The Queen finally found the courage and once again called upon the Slave in the mirror. She searched her heart for her motivations. As the flames began to appear in the mirror, part of her hoped the Slave would not materialise. She didn't really know which scenario would ease her mind: to find him there or not.

And then the Slave appeared in his swirl of purple mist.

"What wouldst thou know, my Queen?"

"Magic Mirror on the wall, who is the fairest one of all?"

"You, my Queen, are the fairest in all the lands, now that Verona has set foot on distant sands."

The Queen felt all the tension flow from her body, and every muscle in her body relaxed. She took a deep breath and sighed. But something within her was still unsettled. What was she becoming? How was it that she chose her own beauty over her dearest companion?

"Slave, I've another question for you," she said.

"I am bound only by honesty, my Queen."

"Perhaps I am fairest in the land. But how is it that I can once again be happy?"

"Happiness is beauty, and beauty is happiness. Beauty brings joy whether possessed by man, woman, girl or boy."

"How I wish that were true," the Queen said.

CHAPTER XIV

INNOCENCE
CHARMED

A day did not go by after Verona's departure when the Queen did not submit to the compulsion to consult the Magic Mirror. Hearing her father tell her how beautiful she was helped lift her spirits. But she felt more alone than ever.

Perhaps it was the loss of her husband and her loneliness that brought her to the mirror each day, but she felt there was something else that compelled her to seek her father's approval and love. Sometimes she felt she had to look in the mirror simply to reassure herself she was in the world. That she was human and not simply a floating grey mist haunting the walls of the castle. She felt real and alive when she looked into the mirror; she felt empowered by her beauty.

No, not just empowered, but invincible.

The Queen's life became a monotonous routine. Each day after she consulted the Magic Mirror, she would retreat to her dungeon. It wasn't until long after the sisters' departure that the Queen had remembered the gift the sisters had spoken of during their last visit. She had been so consumed by the mirror that she thought of little else. But months later, a note arrived from the three reading only:

HOW ARE YOU FARING WITH OUR GIFTS?

The note had reminded the Queen that the sisters had left something for her in the dungeon. Perhaps it was something that might take her mind off of the mirror. Or maybe it was something that possessed a similar power and might only accentuate her magical abilities.

In the dungeon, the Queen discovered a worn old trunk. She opened it and bats flew out at her, and she quickly lifted her cape to guard herself from the sickening beasts. Then she discovered the gifts: books of spells and incantations; vials of strange things, mummy dust, toad eyes, sleep crust; beakers and mortars and pestles. And a cauldron. The Queen quickly became greatly interested in the books, and soon learned how to use them in concert with the strange things the sisters had left behind.

Her first spells were clumsy and didn't work very well, when they worked at all. Early on, she attempted a spell to make her hair, already black, darker than the raven's feather. But instead of transforming her hair to the colour of the bird's wing, it imparted the texture, and the Queen spent days attempting to hide her feather-covered head from the court until she discovered a way to reverse the spell. Another time, she inadvertently dyed her hands green and scarred them with warts. And then she attempted a potion that would make her voice more mellifluous than anyone in the lands, which resulted in her croaking like a toad. When she tried to create an antidote, she sang like a bird and hissed like a serpent, before she at last regained her own voice.

What the citizens of the kingdom assumed to be just another of the Queen's lapses into reclusive sorrow turned out to be week-, then month-, then year-long retreats into her chamber, antechamber, dungeon and the morning room to practise the mystical arts.

Apart from her chambers and the dungeon, she spent a great deal of time up in the parapets, surveying the kingdom. Perhaps searching for anyone, any*thing* that might be a challenge to her beauty.

It should have bewildered the Queen that she had become so closed off, so cold. But she reasoned it was understandable; she never wanted to experience the pain she suffered when she lost her husband. Never again. And she wasn't without everything. In her beauty, she had something that would make people love and admire, perhaps even *fear* her. And she intended to keep it by any and all means at her disposal.

She imagined her heart as a broken mirror, its pieces jingling inside her, a thought that made her feel entirely inhuman. She had become distant with those she once loved. Even her daughter, Snow White, was held at a remove, for the Queen's fear of shattering her heart altogether should anything happen that might rip Snow from her world. She couldn't bring herself to spend more than a few moments in the girl's company. For with every passing year Snow's beauty increased, and the Queen began to feel something other than love for the girl. Something terrible. But she could not think about that.

One early morning, years after the King's death, a knock came at the Queen's door. It was Tilley, the Queen's lady-in-waiting since Verona had been sent away from the court so long ago now. Tilley always spoke quietly, and this, the very thing that Snow loved about the woman, was resented by the Queen, who viewed it as evidence of a weak nature.

"My Queen, where would you like to break your fast?" Tilley asked.

The Queen looked frustrated and Tilley winced in anticipation.

"In the great hall of course, stupid girl. I have been taking my meals in there since you have been here."

Tilley looked distraught.

"What is it, Tilley? Come out with it!" the Queen barked at her.

"It's just that Snow White mentioned wanting to have breakfast in the morning room. She thought it would be a nice change."

The Queen smirked, and she asked the poor girl, "Is Snow White queen of these lands?"

Tilley looked nervous, "No, my Queen. You are, of course."

The Queen went on, "Then please have my meal brought to the great hall and tell Snow White she is expected to break her fast with me."

"Yes, my Queen. I will have one of the women

bring in your bathwater now."

"That will be all, Tilley, thank you."

The Queen wondered how she could be surrounded by such feather-headed women. Surely she wasn't so insolent when she was young. Breakfast in the morning room, indeed!

The Queen emerged from bed, opened her curtains, and looked out on the courtyard. Snow was sitting at the well, the *Queen's* well, feeding the bluebirds. She had become a beautiful young woman. Snow didn't seem to notice, but a handsome young man was riding by on the grounds and stopped his horse so he might look upon her. He seemed spellbound by her loveliness. Indeed, he looked as though he was falling in love right there and then. The Queen shut the curtains with a firm pull and went to her mirror.

"Magic Mirror on the wall, who is the fairest one of all?"

"You, my Queen, are fairest."

The Queen smiled, but something within her felt cold and icy. Something disturbed her about this man approaching Snow White. Jealousy? Was that what had compelled the Queen to rush to the mirror? Was she resenting Snow for her beauty? Her youth? Or was it more benevolent? Was she protecting Snow from love? After all, look where love had left the Queen.

The Queen made her way down to the great hall. She had come to love this room for the very things that caused her discomfort about it when she had first arrived; it was cavernous and commanding. She *felt* like a queen here, and it pleased her to sit regally on the throne while the arched stained-glass windows cast a lovely blue light in the chamber. Snow was sitting to the right of the head of the table looking pure, innocent and beautiful.

The Queen made her way to her seat and stood staring at Snow, who was already seated. She gave the girl a look and nodded to motion that Snow should stand to greet her mother.

Snow hesitated, and then stood, "Good morning, Mother."

"Good morning, Snow."

The Queen took her seat and motioned for Snow to do the same.

"So I hear you would prefer to break your fast in the morning room?" she said.

"Yes, I thought it might make for a nice change; this room is so large just for the two of us. I remember when I was a little girl we would have family meals in the smaller dining hall or in the morning r—"

"Enough!" the Queen snapped.

But inwardly, the Queen recalled how happy those days were. She couldn't bring herself to dine in those rooms now. It hurt her too much without her husband. And Snow, all grown up, the innocent girl becoming a beautiful woman. The Queen looked up at the stone beauty above the mantel. She looked stern and disapproving, as if she were reading the Queen's thoughts.

"I prefer this room, Snow. We have gone over this before. If you'd like to take your meals in the morning room then by all means do so; it matters not to me where you break your fast. But I will not be joining you."

Snow looked disappointed. "I would never see you at all if we took breakfast in different rooms," she said.

"Indeed."

Snow just shook her head.

"I am growing weary of your attitude, Snow White. I won't have you casting such looks at me. I said you could take your meals in any room you desire. What more do you want from me?"

Snow White looked at her mother with sad eyes.

"Nothing, Mother. Never mind."

"Very well then, there is something I've wanted to mention for some while now, I think it is time you take on responsibility. You have no skills to speak of, and as you don't seem to have any suitors we cannot assume you will be married."

Snow looked confounded.

"I've told Tilley to provide you with some working clothes so you may help her with some of the chores around the castle. I think it will do you some good."

"I don't mind helping Tilley. I often do anyway," Snow said.

The Queen went on, "But I won't have you ruining your nice clothes. You should wear something more appropriate to the tasks at hand."

"Of course, Mother."

"Go to Tilley, and she will dress you in rag wear. That will be suitable for the kind of work we'll expect of you."

Snow stood up and left the great hall in a hurry.

The Queen heaved a deep breath. She thought back to herself at the brink of womanhood, and of something Nanny had told her then:

Do not believe your father's lies, my little girl. He doesn't see you as you are and I fear for your soul should you ever let his darkness linger in your heart. You are beautiful, my dear, truly. Don't ever forget that, even if I am not here to remind you.

She had always been beautiful and now her father, whose spirit was captured within the mirror, was bound to tell the truth. The Queen felt an immense power in that. She got up from the table, went through the arched doorway, then proceeded down the hall and stopped at the tapestry with the image of a large apple blossom tree filled with blackbirds. She remembered the story she had told Snow so many years ago about the woman who could turn into a dragon. She now felt much like that woman, isolated and alone, so different from anyone she knew. She moved the tapestry to the side and revealed a passageway leading to the dungeon.

As the Queen made her way down the stairs, she dragged her hand across the stone walls. They felt cold and hard to her touch, and she liked that. She opened the windows to give the room some air and saw a large black crow sitting on the ledge.

She had not been spending as much time in the dungeon as she had when she first discovered the books and potions, when it was all new. But she still spent many of her late afternoons and evenings there. Over time, she had become more familiar with the sisters' books and the spells inside. Many of them kept her looking young and fair. But she'd recently been experimenting with some other kinds of spells. She had beauty and power. But she wanted more.

The books and spells had been intimidating, and alien when she first dabbled in them. But now their dusty leather covers, some embossed with silver death's-heads, others clearly marked for which aspect of magic was detailed within, looked less sinister and more beautiful.

She recalled how clumsy her first spells were. Now, the books were as familiar as old friends.

"Striking blackbirds that searched the skies, bringing her news from the outside world," the Queen said, recalling the story she told Snow that rainy evening so long ago.

A crow hopped in the window as if summoned and looked at her with its yellow eyes. She decided to let him stay and keep her company while she read the sisters' books.

Then, a voice called out to her from above.

"Excuse me? My Queen, are you down here? It's quite urgent!"

The Queen was angry at herself for ever telling Tilley where she was spending her afternoons. True, the chamber she was in was remote, but that did not mean that a nosy visitor wouldn't stumble upon her laboratory. She would immediately have one of the workmen install a sturdier door with a stronger bolt to seal off the dungeon chamber.

"Yes, Tilley, I will be right up."

The Queen patted the crow on its head and then ascended the stairs to see what the fuss was all about.

Tilley looked unusually distressed.

"What is it, then?" the Queen asked.

Tilley just stood, shaking, unable to speak.

"Come out with it, girl!"

The servant finally found her voice. "It's Snow White, she was helping me fetch water from the well and somehow she... she... toppled over the edge!"

The Queen rushed out of the room and into the courtyard where she found Snow laying on the ground, soaked and unconscious. A distressed young man, the same one the Queen had seen riding on the grounds, was bending over her body. Now that she saw him up close she recognised him as a young prince from a neighbouring land.

The Queen turned her attention to her daughter's limp form, and her heart stopped. Her mother, her husband, and now her daughter, *dead*. The Queen was paralysed with fear and grief. And then Snow began to cough. Water spilled from her ruby red lips, and she blinked open her eyes.

"Thank the gods!" the Queen said, clutching her hands to her chest and embracing the girl.

The Prince looked utterly relieved. He placed his hand on her cheek tenderly and said, "Thank goodness you're alive."

Snow looked up at him with her father's eyes, *good* eyes, and said, "Thank you."

She was clearly smitten with this young man.

The Queen stepped in and said, "Thank you, young sir, but I will take over from here."

"Of course, my lady, may I call again tomorrow afternoon to check on the fair maiden?"

The Queen could tell he was falling in love with her.

"Perhaps, if she is up to it. Tilley will take you round the back end of the courtyard if you would like to refresh yourself before you depart. Thank you for your assistance."

Then the Queen grabbed Snow by the arm and whisked her away into the castle.

CHAPTER XV

A RETURN

It had been months since Snow White's accident at the well, and the young Prince who had saved her had come to visit several times. That morning in the garden, while Snow was off helping Tilley, the Prince asked for an audience with the Queen. The Queen knew he would ask for Snow's hand in marriage. Before he could even make his request, the Queen wanted to make it as clear as possible that he wasn't to return to the castle. So she quickly decided she would put the issue to rest immediately.

"I am trying to spare your feelings, young man,

but you've put me in a very uncomfortable situation where I fear I must be nothing but perfectly frank. Snow White does not love you, and I can not let my daughter marry someone she does not love," she said.

The Prince looked crestfallen.

"I can see you thought otherwise. I'm sorry, dear Prince. Perhaps she was sparing your feelings; she really should have been honest with you," the Queen said.

The Prince left without another word. The Queen would tell Snow White that the Prince had left a note saying that he did not love her and that he wanted to end their courtship before Snow thought he felt more deeply for her than he really did. She had done the right thing, even if it meant lying to them both. Even if it broke their hearts now, it was nothing compared to losing each other to tragedy, betrayal or death. But she couldn't help but feel wicked, too. And that terrified and comforted her all at once.

Somewhere in her heart she knew her motivations were also fuelled by jealously. She was envious that Snow should have someone to love her and she should not. How could she stand there and watch them pledge themselves to each other in love when her love was walled away?

And what would the King think of his Queen now? She sometimes imagined that he was looking upon her from wherever he was, judging her for what had become her wicked ways. She felt that something else within her was taking over, and that she no longer had any ability to control her own actions.

But no, Snow White would thank her one day for sparing her heartache. She would understand.

The Queen rushed to her chamber and went again to the mirror. She needed comfort and she received it. As usual, she was fairest.

But when the Queen looked at herself in the mirror, she didn't seem like the same woman. Yes, she was beautiful, but there was something different about her eyes. There was a harshness to her beauty; it was cold and removed. She thought that it added an elegance and majesty to her demeanour, something a queen should possesses. But it didn't quell her fears that she was losing herself in grief, fear and most of all, vanity.

Her only comfort it seemed was her Slave, her father, whom she had grown to trust in her years of solitude. She asked him, "Do I seem much changed to you?"

"Indeed, my Queen, you do," he said.

"How so?" she asked.

"You are stately, queenly and elegant."

"Do I seem cold to you?" the Queen asked.

"No, my Queen, you are not cold, you have simply matured into a distinguished woman of high station. You are the Queen and cannot be bothered with matters of the heart."

Matters of the heart? It seemed not long ago that her heart ruled her. But now, ruling a kingdom in solitude, her heart seemed all but lost. As if her thoughts were open to him, the man in the mirror continued, "A woman of your stature cannot be governed by her emotions, lest she be unable to handle the tasks at hand."

And with that advice she went about the business of the day.

But she soon faced something she was not expecting.

Tilley came running down a corridor. "My Queen," she shouted, smiling. "A party has arrived!"

"I was not expecting anyone. Ask them to leave," the Queen said bitterly.

But before Tilley could give her command, someone had entered the hall.

"It has been so long since I've last seen you, Majesty. I have missed you these many long years."

The Queen felt a flood of emotion. Verona. She quickly checked herself in a hall mirror to allay any fears that she looked ragged. The Queen's poor shattered heart leaped, and then quickly sank. She did not know what to make of this visit.

Verona had fallen in love on her mission and been married to a lord.

The Queen felt that emotion which had now become familiar to her; a mix of joy and jealousy for her friend.

A Return

They had been so very close at one time, and now she wondered how she had gone so many years without Verona's company and friendship. The thought of it confounded her, but she buried it deep within herself, resolute not to let her love weaken her sense of strength.

Despite her relief to have Verona out of the kingdom, she had missed her so much, especially during those first few months after her departure. She felt icy and horrid when she thought of it, sending her dearest friend away for the sake of vanity and selfishness. Seeing Verona in the castle reawakened something in the Queen, something human and warm. Yes, she was happy to have her friend back in her company.

The Queen arranged a splendid evening just for the two of them in the great hall. The room was glowing with candles, and the table filled with rich, savoury foods that she knew were Verona's favourites. The meal was wonderful, but the conversation was awkward. What does one talk about with an old friend after one has sufficiently reminisced?

After their meal the two ladies retired to the sitting room where they enjoyed fine spirits, which helped the conversation along.

"I regret sending you away, Verona," the Queen said, though in truth only part of her regretted it. "Had I the opportunity to make the decision again, I do not believe I would send you from this court."

"Oh, but then I never would have met my lord. I am grateful to you, Majesty. You have brought immense happiness into my life, and I thank you for that," Verona said.

"You love him, then, this husband of yours?" asked the Queen.

"Yes, of course, why would you ask such a question?" Verona said.

"I am just looking after your heart, my dear friend, that is all. It would distress me to see you hurt by the loss of him. He is away on campaign, is he not? You should prepare yourself for his death."

"I shall not! Why would you even say such

a thing?" Verona said, standing up from her comfortable chair.

"Because this is life, my dear Verona. It is our lot to lose our loves and feel our hearts break in the wake of that loss. I would shield you from it if I could, my friend, but there was nothing anyone could have said to prepare me for the breaking of my soul when the King passed from my life."

Verona's eyes were filled with sadness. "I remember that day well, my Queen, and my heart goes out to you, it does; but I cannot live in fear of losing him, for fear of not living my life at all. May I speak frankly with you, Majesty?"

"Yes, please feel free to speak candidly as you always have, Verona. You are an old friend and that does have its privileges," the Queen said coolly.

"You seem much changed to me, Majesty. You are more beautiful than ever, but something within you has shifted. I fear for your unhappiness and solitude." Verona continued, "Snow White has written to me several times, expressing her concern over you. She is worried that you are so closed off from her. She loves you so much, Majesty, and it breaks my heart to think of you both alone in your grief when you have each other for solace and strength."

"Snow knows how dear she is to me, Verona. I would perish without her," the Queen said.

"Why, then, do you never seek her company? Snow is a remarkable young lady, Majesty. Even now, after these many years of near-abandonment, she would still be a great friend to you, if only you extended your hand," Verona pleaded.

"You dare imply that I have abandoned my daughter?" the Queen snapped.

"Forgive me, Your Majesty, I thought I could speak honestly with you."

"So I said, but it breaks my heart, Verona, to hear these words. You do not know what it is to feel your heart break in the wake of tragedy, and you should pray you never do!"

Verona shook her head. "Please, my Queen and my *friend*. Please go to your daughter, she is not long for this court, as she is approaching the proper marrying age, and I would not see her go from this kingdom without knowing her mother's love."

Her mother's love. The words resonated with the Queen. She had abandoned Snow White for magic mirrors and spell books from the strange sisters. Was she so mad, so deranged by the loss of her husband, that she should be too afraid to love her daughter for fear of losing her? This was madness, surely! And why did it take Verona's words to make her see this clearly for the first time? She should have never sent her friend, this woman she once called a sister, from court to go so long without her companionship, without her council and her love. Perhaps much could have been averted if Verona were here these many long years.

Then the Queen found something stir within her that she had not felt in a great while. Her shattered heart felt suddenly mended.

"I would be much pleased if you extended your stay, Verona. Please say you will remain here for the entirety of your husband's campaign. I have been without your company for too long, and I do not wish to see you go from me again so quickly."

"Yes, of course, Majesty, I would be happy to stay in court with you and Snow White."

"Thank you, Verona. Shall we make a picnic in the woods tomorrow, like old times, the three of us?"

"That would be lovely, Your Majesty. I'm sure that will make Snow very happy, too."

"Very well, then," the Queen answered. "We shall leave that dolt Tilley behind. Never in my life have I been met with such incompetence."

The Queen laughed, and Verona laughed along. But it was no longer the laughter of camaraderie. The Queen's laugh was one of power and disdain, and Verona's was uncomfortable.

That evening, while the Queen was alone in her chamber, she began to feel restless. She had already questioned the Slave today. But that was before Verona had returned.

She needed to call on him again.

She needed to know.

She stumbled through the darkened room,

approached the Magic Mirror, and summoned the Slave. Then she asked her question.

"I cannot determine who is fairest with Verona at court, my Queen," the Slave responded. "Your beauty is so close. Elements of hers almost surpass your own. While elements of yours nearly eclipse hers."

The Queen fought the impulse to banish Verona, even to *kill* her. The urge was powerful, but the Queen found an old strength within her, forged around friendship and love, that allowed her to fight harder.

She ripped the curtains from her windows and wrapped them around the mirror. Then she called for Uncle Marcus's good friend, the Huntsman. He was perhaps the strongest man in the court and could easily perform the task she had at hand. He arrived quickly and she pushed the mirror towards him.

"Take this with you and bury it deep within the forest. Leave no marker to its whereabouts, and never, no matter how I implore you, *never* tell me where you have buried it, this part is paramount, *never tell me where you have buried it!* Do you understand?"

"Yes, my Queen," the Huntsman replied.

"And tell absolutely no one of this conversation or where you have hidden it, and whatever you do, do not seek to know what is wrapped in this cloth. I will know if you have deceived me in any way."

"I would never deceive you, my Queen. Never. I only wish to seek your favour," the Huntsman said, bowing.

The Queen watched from her window as the Huntsman rode away on a two-horse carriage, with the Magic Mirror wrapped and stowed in the rear. The Huntsman vanished into the forest, taking with him the thing that had bolstered the Queen since her greatest loss, but which had also become her greatest weakness.

CHAPTER XVI

TORMENT

Having Verona at court should have been a great comfort to the Queen, but she couldn't keep her mind from drifting to the Magic Mirror or its location, and this made her especially bothered and easily agitated.

It was madness that she should be so consumed. Surely if she asked the Huntsman he would have little choice other than to follow her orders. Perhaps after some persuading, he would reveal the location. But would she subject herself to that torment, the knowledge that she was too weak-minded to keep herself from the mirror? And would she have the

189

Huntsman know of this weakness as well?

The days that followed were pure agony. The Queen was so caught up in her need of the Magic Mirror that she was haunted even in her dreams, leaving her sleepless and ill. Every day that she was parted from the mirror, she seemed to become sicklier, so much so that she often felt near to death.

She often woke terrified to a dream that dominated her restless slumber...

In the dream she was in the forest, frantically searching for the mirror. The canopy of trees obscured the sky, leaving her alone in darkness and in fear. The sisters were there, too, coming and going, and changing shape and form, the way things do in dreams. The Queen would come upon a freshly disturbed mound of dirt and begin digging with her bare hands. Desperate to find the mirror, she would dig for what felt like an eternity, her hands bleeding, her body weak, and her mind spinning out of control. Finally, she would feel something soft and wet covered in cloth. After unwrapping it she would discover there, in the cloth, a heart, its blood pouring all over her hands.

"Momma?" she would hear. It would be Snow, a young girl once again, standing there with a look of terrible sadness on her little face, her white dressing gown covered in blood, dripping from where her heart once was. Her face blank; her eyes hollow and blackened, her skin ashen and her expression reproachful. The sisters were always about, giggling their eerie laughter. The Queen would move to scream, but no sound would come, she was so paralysed with fear.

Every morning she woke, soaked in sweat, anxious from this exact dream, or a similar one. It sent a tremor through her and made her feel weak. She had no control over her own will.

She felt defeated.

One evening she dreamed of the sisters. "Over there!" they called, standing in the forest, appearing and disappearing under the moonless, midnight sky. "Dig—here—the—Magic—Mirror—your—Slave—" They chattered and laughed, and the moon illuminated their ghastly doll-like faces with a pale blue glow.

And when she awoke the morning after this

dream, she found something wrapped in soiled cloth sitting on the floor beside her bed. Her hands, too, were covered in earth, and her nightdress was tattered and caked with mud.

She thought she must still have been dreaming. Or, had she gone into the forest in search of the mirror while she slept? For the first time in more than a week she felt renewed, her strength coming back to her and her sense of self returning. She unwrapped the large object and there, staring back at her, was her reflection. She collapsed on top of the mirror and embraced it like a lost lover returned.

Something within her had changed. Verona was right. She wasn't the same woman who had married the King those many years ago; she was something wholly different and it frightened her. But it also gave her a sense of strength and of power. She would never be parted from the Magic Mirror again. Her life, her *soul*, seemed dependent upon it. She tore open the cloth that covered the mirror revealing its face.

"Magic Mirror on the wall, who is the fairest one of all?"

"Your beauty is beyond compare, but Verona is fairest."

"Perhaps then," the Queen said, smiling wickedly, "it is time for her to go."

CHAPTER XVII

ANOTHER FAREWELL

The next morning, the Queen was breaking her fast with Verona in the morning room when the Huntsman brought Snow White in. She looked tattered, her rags soiled and torn more than usual, and her face was badly bruised.

"What's happened?" the Queen asked as she stood from her seat almost knocking over a teapot.

"My horse was spooked, I couldn't control him."

The Huntsman interrupted Snow, "She was riding Lurid, my Queen, the new stallion. I warned her he wasn't fit to ride, but she took him out while I was hunting."

The Queen raged, "You could have *died*, Snow! What were you thinking riding by yourself?" Snow didn't answer.

"You *were* alone, were you not?"

Snow looked at her shoes.

"You were with *him*? After I *expressly* forbade you to ever see him again?"

Snow dropped her head in admission.

"Leave now, before I strike you; I cannot even look at you!" the Queen shouted.

Snow stood her ground. "He told me what you said, Mother! You lied to him, you said I didn't love him. How *could* you?"

The Queen slapped Snow square in the face.

Verona looked horrified.

"My Queen, please!" Verona shouted.

The Queen whipped her head round like an angry viper and snapped at Verona, "Silence!"

Snow was in tears, sobbing so hard she couldn't speak. Verona went to her side and wrapped her arms around her.

"I don't even know who you are anymore," Verona said bitterly to the Queen. "You have become a cold, wicked woman, and there is nothing of the friend I once loved within you."

"Then you will have no trouble with my banishing you from this kingdom, *dear* Verona. Forever. And I have a mind to banish that incorrigible child along with you. But there is a life for her here. This castle has a use for her. The horse's stalls have never been so clean. The outhouses have never smelled so fresh," the Queen said sardonically.

"Majesty..." the Huntsman began.

"Silence! Or you will suffer the same fate," the Queen barked at him.

Snow buried her face in the Huntsman's chest and sobbed. He ushered her out of the room and Verona followed close behind. Then Verona asked the servants to gather her belongings, and after bidding goodbye to the familiar faces around the court she hadn't seen in years, she left the castle.

The Queen watched her go, then quickly retreated to her chamber. She went to the mirror, but she feared the Slave's reply. She couldn't bring herself to ask him. She couldn't bear hearing that she wasn't the fairest, not this evening. So she retired to bed. And the next morning she awoke feeling a new rush of energy. Verona was far away from court. She was sure the Slave in the mirror would put her heart at ease.

"Magic Mirror, on the wall, who is the fairest one of all?"

"You are, my Queen..."

The Queen felt uneasy.

"I sense hesitation in your voice, Slave. Speak to me," the Queen said.

"You are the fairest, Majesty. But do not ask me to advise on the state of your heart."

The Queen spat upon the mirrored glass, then whipped up her cape and stormed from the room as the Slave in the Magic Mirror disappeared in a cloud of purple smoke.

CHAPTER XVIII

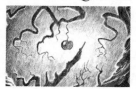

DREAM SICKNESS

"*Show me Snow White!*"

Snow White was running in the dark forest, full of fear and anguish. She was panic-stricken, alone, and heading back to the castle. Back to her stepmother, who would surely have the Huntsman punished for attempting to hurt her, and weaving lies that she plotted her own daughter's death.

"Foolish girl."

The forest came alive; it was visceral and dangerous. It wanted Snow White's life. The Queen's rage penetrated the trees, bringing their leafless limbs to life. As if they were hands, the tree branches scratched and grabbed at Snow, entrapping her, pinning her to the ground. They wrapped themselves around her neck, choking her and clawing at her chest for her heart. The forest would do what the Huntsman could not. Snow's eyes filled with terror, she cried out, "Momma, please help me!" The Queen's heart melted in that moment. The trees released Snow White from their clutches.

The girl ran deep into the forest, where the trees obscured the sky completely. She was in pure darkness, surrounded by glowing eyes peering at her menacingly. She was alone in fear, and she ran, not knowing if the path would take her to safety or to death. The Queen's magic could not go where Snow wandered. She escaped out of the forest and out of the Queen's view.

The Queen jolted awake. She felt a freezing chill and desired nothing but the warm comfort of her bed. She stayed there for days, conjuring only the energy to make a daily visit to the Magic Mirror, and an occasional walk to the window to make sure Snow White was scrubbing away at the castle, and avoiding that meddlesome Prince.

Even from afar, she noticed how beautiful Snow

had become. Not only in outward appearance but, like her father, in her pure heart. It would not be long before… No, the Queen could not permit herself to think it.

She felt alone, forsaken by her husband, and now Snow was away from her as well. No, that was a dream. Or was it? Everything in her life seemed to be tangled up now: dreams and reality, fantasy and nightmares. She felt that she had become something other than human, something completely alien to herself. She wondered if her father had lived his days in such a state. These days she saw much of him within herself.

Late one night she woke with her nightdress soaked in sweat; she felt weak and every part of her ached. She got up and poured some water into her washing bowl to cool herself when she noticed something upon the floor. It was blood, pools of it, mingling with footprints, leading from the Queen's bedside out her chamber door. The Queen took a torch for light and followed the bloody trail out the castle and into the forest.

The forest was blackened, as if ravaged by a fire; there was no light from the moon or stars. It was a dead place, ruined by her jealousy and hate. The only source of light was the torch she carried. The bloody trail finally ended. A heart was clasped within the clawlike branches of a dead tree, looking like a strange, bleeding fruit, blood glistening on the branches in the torchlight. The Queen just stood there, feeling empty and alone, terror gripping her own heart.

"Momma?" The Queen turned with a start.

Standing there was Snow, a child once more. Her face whiter than death, her eyes black holes, and her white dress covered in blood. "Momma, can I please have my heart back?"

The Queen screamed. What had she done?

"Your Majesty, please wake up! You're having a nightmare," Tilley insisted.

"My little girl needs me. She came here last night... because she needs me! The forest took her heart!"

Her chambermaid just looked at her, bewildered.

"No, my Queen, Snow White is in the courtyard; she's fine."

"But the blood on the floor! It's there, see!"

"You must have broken something in the night and stepped on the glass. Majesty, you've been ill."

"No, it is Snow White's blood. She came here in the night, I swear!"

"Look at your feet, Majesty, they're filthy and *bleeding*. You're sick, please go back to sleep, you need your rest."

"Leave me alone, you idiotic wench."

"But, Your Majesty, I should tend to your—"

"I said *leave!*"

The Queen stared at the blood and glass on her chamber floor. Snow had come to her in the night, she knew it! Her little girl was lost and alone and searching for her heart. Although she had been doing little more than sleeping these past few days, she passed out from exhaustion once more.

* * *

"You must kill Snow White if you want to survive, if you desire your beauty back."

She would rather rid herself of the mirror and let herself die.

"If Snow White lives, it will be slow and painful, daughter. You would linger unto death for many years, your soul rotting away within you, withering your body to a husk; everyone will look upon you with pity and disgust. You will wish for death and feel no release even after they have buried you deep within the ground. The magic of the mirror, the spells of the sisters, will keep you alive even in the darkness. You will suffer for death, feel the need for it, want to seek it out, but your body will not be able to enforce your will. You will be trapped within yourself, alone and in agony."

"Why are you doing this?"

"I've hated you from the day you came into this world."

"All of this was lies then? Why?"

"Revenge, for your mother's death, for the breaking of my soul."

The Queen woke again, remembering her

father's words from her dream. She remembered saying similar words to Verona about the loss of her husband. She was feverish and ill, and her mind wasn't her own. Why were these thoughts invading her? She fought against them but couldn't help but feel that she had wasted her life, for vain wishes and a love her father never had for her. And now she was going to be forced to kill her daughter.

No, that was a dream. The mirror had no hold over her.

Her mind was muddled; she couldn't determine reality from nightmares and found that she was unable to keep herself awake, instead falling back into her fevered dreamscape…

She was looking into her mirror, "I am like you, Father. I have forsaken my daughter. I despise her beauty."

"You have always been like me. A part of me lives within you; you share my blood. We are bound by that and by the magic of the mirror. Part of my soul is in you."

"We own your soul," the sisters' voices came. "If your soul is in her, she is ours as well. Just as your wife was, before we took her!"

Dream Sickness

"No one owns me!" the Queen shouted.

The sisters laughed, then faded away.

The Queen stumbled out of her chamber feeling numb and walked the familiar path she and Snow White used to wander when Snow was still a little girl. Time had completely gotten away from her and she ended up walking much farther than she had intended. She was in the Dead Wood again. Everything was blackened and it reeked of sulphur. She had done this. Her hate and fear not only ruined this forest but the entirety of her life. Everything was lost to her now. Out of the corner of her eye she saw something green and red in the black emptiness. It was a bright, shiny apple hanging from a tree in this Dead Wood. She wondered how she hadn't noticed it right away, it looked remarkable and uncanny among the dead trees. Something about it gave her hope. She took the brilliant apple from the dead tree, put it into the folds of her simple dress, and pulled her shawl over her head and made her way to a tiny cottage deep within the woods.

As the Queen woke from her feverish dream, Tilley was putting a cool washcloth to her head.

"I need something to eat. An… an apple," the

Queen muttered through parched lips.

Tilley took the cloth from the Queen's forehead and placed it in a bowl of cool rosewater.

"You've been dreaming, my Queen." And she went on, "Snow is outside and would like to see you."

The Queen almost turned her away, but then thought better of it.

"Yes, ask her to come in."

Tilley called to the attendant by the door and Snow White entered the room. She was so beautiful. The sun seemed to follow her wherever she went. The rags she wore only accentuated her beauty by contrasting it with their raggedness. She was so young, so sweet, so *fair*.

"I'm sorry you're so ill, Mother. Is there anything I can do for you?"

"There is. Please, would you please find me an apple? The reddest and shiniest you can find?" the Queen asked, as Tilley continued to wipe down her forehead.

Snow looked to the chambermaid who returned her weary look.

"Of course, Mother, I will pick you an apple if you'd like," Snow White said.

"Thank you, my little bird," replied the Queen, drifting in and out of her dream state.

The Queen came to a large moss-covered tree where she knew a sleep-inducing root would grow, because it thrived in dark and dampness. Feeling icy and wicked, she dug in the earth. The root was there as she had thought. She took out her little dagger and cut the root open; its oils spilled out all over her hands, reminding her of blood. She felt evil, a chill coming over her. What had caused her to commit such foul acts? She rubbed the oily substance from the root onto the apple. It would make Snow sleep, a deathlike sleep. Perhaps the Queen should take a bite of the apple, too, and then she could be with her daughter without fear of hurting her.

She ventured through the forest and came to a clearing in the wood, and there were gathered the sisters.

"So—"

"You have discovered—"

"The poison apple, have you?"

Then, the sisters took the Queen by her arms and dragged her to the far end of the clearing. The Magic Mirror was there, and Lucinda held the Queen in front of it, while Martha and Ruby stood alongside, gawking at the Queen's reflection.

Her face, her beautiful face, melted into a wrinkled old mess, lined with the marks of age and dotted with warts. She could smell her own breath and it was foul, befitting her rotting teeth. She was a hag, an old, vile, disgusting witch.

The sisters laughed as the Queen tore away from them. It was difficult for her to run, since her back was now hunched in this new body.

She ran and ran through the forest, as fast as her legs would carry her. And then she came to a cottage. Snow was there. But she would not recognise her now.

The girl, a woman now, was so beautiful. But something was wrong, she didn't seem her vibrant self, something within her had changed. In that moment, the Queen understood. She had taken her heart. Not physically. No, she still lived. But the Queen had taken her daughter's spirit when she had forsaken her. Snow was talking to stray animals; she seemed to have many of them about the cottage and within. She wondered if the ordeal had made Snow's mind unsound; the thought crushed her heart. The Queen wondered if even in this state, looking like an old hag and Snow White delirious *with fear and grief, the girl might recognise her. Something in Snow's eyes told her she did.*

But it wasn't possible.

Holding a little bird in her hand, Snow smiled at the old woman with that little smile of hers. She looked like a child again. A beautiful child. A beautiful woman. Surely, more beautiful than the Queen.

"Hello, my dear, how are you today?"

Snow White just stood there staring at her as if mesmerised. "I have a gift for you, my sweet," said the Queen, handing the apple to her daughter. Snow looked into her mother's eyes as she took the apple.

Snow White took a bite almost absent-mindedly and then quickly fell to the ground, the apple still in her hand. And just before she closed her eyes she said, "But my dream has already come true, Momma. You came for me as I knew you would. I love you…"

The Queen bent down and kissed her daughter and whispered in her ear, "Oh, I love you, too, my little bird. I love you so much."

CHAPTER XIX

A Foul
Possession

The Queen rose from her bed feeling better than she had in a long while. She felt strength, power and a surge of confidence. True, her dream proved that she was conflicted and that she had lost her way. But the memory of Snow as she looked in the dreams: sickly, pale, dead, stuck with her. But instead of warming her heart to rush to her daughter and embrace her, happy that she lived, the images served only to renew the Queen's spirits.

How could such a child, one with hollow black eyes, one without a heart, possibly rival the Queen's beauty?

A Foul Possession

She began to wonder how her mind could have been so plagued with such weakness and sentiment. She had been ill. Simple. She got up from her bed for the first time in many days, opened her curtains, and saw Snow White at the wishing well, scrubbing away in her rags. She was fair, no doubt. But nowhere near as fair as the Queen.

She called on her attendants to draw a bath, and was soon refreshed and outfitted in her finest gown. Her crown sat neatly upon her covered raven hair, and her favourite purple-and-black cape was fastened to her gown with a gold-and-ruby pendant.

She examined herself in the Magic Mirror and smiled. Truly, she had never looked more beautiful.

"Slave in the Magic Mirror," she began, "come from the farthest space, through wind and darkness, I summon thee, speak! Let me see thy face!"

Flames filled the mirror, then subsided, revealing the face in the Magic Mirror.

"What wouldst thou know, my Queen?"

"Magic Mirror on the wall, who is the fairest one of all?"

"Famed is thy beauty, Majesty, but hold! A lovely maid I see! Rags cannot hide her gentle grace, alas, she is more fair than thee," the Slave said.

"A lash for her!" the Queen shouted, incensed. Who could this woman be? "Reveal her name!" the Queen ordered.

"Lips as red as a rose, hair black as ebony, skin white as snow…"

The Queen felt faint. The room began to sway, and she nearly lost her footing. She clasped her hand around her brooch and recoiled in horror.

"Snow White!" she said.

She rushed to the window. Snow was still scrubbing away at the steps by the well. While she did this she sang and danced, and the Queen felt something very near hatred for the girl. Nothing, it seemed, could dampen Snow White's spirits. How could the girl have recovered so well from the loss of her father? Did she not remember all the happy times they had had together? How could she find it in her heart to smile, to laugh and to sing?

To *love*?

A Foul Possession

The Queen noticed the young Prince step up beside Snow White. Snow quickly jumped up and ran from the Prince, no doubt fearing the wrath of the Queen, who warned her against cavorting with the boy. This satisfied the Queen briefly, until Snow White quickly reappeared on the balcony below her and began to sing along with the Prince, who was now sickeningly serenading her. Not only was the girl surpassing the Queen as the fairest in the land, but she had found herself in love. An insult to both her father and the Queen!

The Queen quickly closed the curtains and started when she turned to find the three sisters standing in her chamber.

"You three! How have you come to be here?"

"We have our ways, Majesty—" Lucinda said.

"And you have yours," Ruby finished.

"What do you want?" the Queen asked bitterly.

"The question is—" Martha asked.

"What do *you* want?" Lucinda finished.

"I think you already know the answer, dears," the Queen said.

The sisters began speaking, picking up one another's sentences.

"The power is yours, Majesty. The answers you seek are in the volumes we left here long ago, tomes on the Black Arts, poisons and potions, disguises. If you know where they reside, you will have your answer. After all, you come from a long line of witches. The power is not only in those books, it is in your blood, as it was in your mother's."

"Liars!" the Queen said, hurling a delicate vase at the sisters.

"Oh dear me," Lucinda said.

"You've developed a temper," Martha finished.

"That could come in handy in your current circumstance," Lucinda said.

"See, there is an easier way to reclaim your post as fairest," Ruby continued.

"And what would that be?" the Queen asked sceptically.

"Kill the girl," the sisters said in tandem and broke into their sickly cackle.

"Kill Snow White? You are mad!" the Queen

said. But part of her had already been contemplating the same fate for the girl.

The sisters continued their sniggering. "Madness is in the mind of the beholder, Queen.

"It is the only way. She must die either by your hand or someone else's. Wouldn't you want to be the apple of your father's eye again? Do you not want to hear the Slave tell you that *you* are fairest?"

"Of course, but—"

"Your Uncle Marcus's friend, the Huntsman. Order him—" Lucinda said.

"To do the deed," Ruby finished. "Your husband—"

"Will be avenged of his daughter's rebuking his memory for happiness with that other royal man, and you will again have your rightful—"

"Place as fairest in the lands."

"And best of all, her blood won't be on your hands."

The sisters broke into a cackle again.

The Queen shook her head. It might have looked as though she were disagreeing with the sisters, but in truth, she was fighting the urge within herself to submit to their suggestion.

"It seems as if you need—" Lucinda said.

"A bit of help," Ruby finished.

Martha opened her pouch and produced an empty teacup.

Lucinda said, "Metal and ore, goodness no more."

She bent down and spat into the cup.

"Love and tenderness, flee; instead, here, have a piece of me," Ruby said, leaning over Martha's shoulder and also spitting into the cup.

"From a queen in pain, to a queen who reigns," Martha said, lifting the cup to her shrivelled lips and spitting in it as well.

The sisters then each waved a hand over the cup, and when the Queen could see it once again she noticed it was filled with steaming liquid.

"Drink," Lucinda said.

The Queen looked sceptical, but took the cup. If it would help strengthen her, which is what she gathered from the incantation, then she would happily accept it.

As the liquid moved down her throat into her body, she felt an unbelievable rage. But it was a strange, focused kind of rage that she felt could be wielded as a weapon. It seemed that her body had been completely taken over by the part of her she'd been fighting for so long. And she found that she loved it.

"Sisters," the Queen said evilly. "Leave me. Now. Or I will see to it that each of you is disemboweled and your entrails hung in the trees that flank this castle. The rest of your remains will be fed to the beasts in the castle moat."

Lucinda smiled darkly, and Ruby and Martha followed suit.

"Call us if you need us, dear," Lucinda said. And the three disappeared as mysteriously as they had arrived.

CHAPTER XX

THE HUNTSMAN

"Has the Huntsman returned?" the Queen asked Tilley, who she had ordered to her room.

"No, Your Majesty, not yet. However he should be back anytime now, I should think. It is approaching midday," the servant replied.

"Send him to me the moment he arrives; tell him not to bother making himself presentable. I understand he will want to after a long day of stalking, but it is of the gravest importance I see him at once."

"Yes, my Queen."

And with that, Tilley left the chamber. The

Queen was too nervous to eat. She wanted desperately to approach the mirror again, to ask who was fairest, to hear her father say it was she, but she knew that would not be the answer. The thought of once again hearing Snow White was fairest ground her stony heart to dust. She paced. She waited. Soon, she would once again be the fairest in the land... once Snow White was dead. Time went slowly; she looked at the faces of the beastly women on either side of her hearth; she imagined herself transformed into a dragon and killing Snow White herself. If only her power was that great.

She sat down on her throne and awaited the Huntsman's arrival.

And then there came a knock on her chamber door.

"Come!" she called.

It was the Huntsman. He looked rugged and dirty, with earth sticking to his sweaty brow.

"You called for me, my Queen?"

"Indeed. I would like you to take Snow White away from here. Take her far into the forest. Find some secluded glade where she can pick wildflowers—"

"Yes, Your Majesty," the Huntsman said.

"And there, my faithful Huntsman, you will kill her," the Queen said.

"But, Your Majesty! The little princess!" the Huntsman pleaded.

"Silence! You know the penalty if you fail!" the Queen said.

"Yes, Your Majesty," the Huntsman said, dropping his eyes to the floor. It was the child's life or his own. Or worse, the lives of his family.

The Queen went on, "But to make doubly sure you do not fail, bring back her heart in this."

The Queen lifted an ornately carved wooden box and thrust it forward to present it to the Huntsman. It was the beautifully decorated one with a heart pierced by a sword as a lock. A testament to just how much the Queen had transformed, how much she had lost sight of the things that were once dear to her, was that she did not even recognise it as the dowry box of the King's first wife. The very box that once contained the letters from Snow's mother.

"Do not fail me!" the Queen commanded.

"I would not, Your Majesty."

The Huntsman left the chamber and the Wicked Queen watched from the window as Snow White was led happily away. The Queen grinned evilly. Then the waiting began.

She paced in her room for hours. She thought she might approach the Magic Mirror, but did not want to do so prematurely. She couldn't bear to hear once more that she was not the fairest one of all.

It was now twilight, and the Huntsman still had not returned. She feared he had lost his nerve and ran off with the child in tow. And then the Wicked Queen heard a knock at the door.

The Huntsman stood there, looking stunned. He handed the Queen the box. He had brought Snow White's heart, just as the Queen had demanded. The Queen felt a perverse thrill of excitement. The old fears and weaknesses did not disturb her thoughts, didn't temper this elation. She had made the right choice in killing the girl. It was for the good of all their family. It felt liberating. And most important, she was once again the most beautiful maiden in all the land.

"Thank you, my loyal man; you will be rewarded greatly for this, I assure you. Now leave me," the Queen said.

The Huntsman left without a word, and the Queen went directly to the mirror. She had been waiting for this.

"Magic Mirror on the wall, who *now* is the fairest one of all?" she asked, with a smirk on her lips and the box containing the heart in her hands.

The Slave appeared and spoke. "Over the Seven Jewelled Hills, beyond the seventh fall, in the cottage of the Seven Dwarfs dwells Snow White, the fairest one of all."

The Queen could not suppress a wicked smile.

"Snow White lies dead in the forest. The Huntsman has brought me proof. Behold, her heart!"

The Queen opened the box and lifted it to the Magic Mirror.

"Snow White still lives," the Slave said. "The fairest in the land. 'Tis the heart of a pig you have in your hand."

"The heart of a pig! Then I have been tricked!" the Queen said.

The Queen flew into a rage so violent the servants below thought the castle might be coming down around them. She stormed down the stairs, through the front doors, into the courtyard and the stables, where the Huntsman was unsaddling his horse.

"You didn't kill her!"

"No, Your Majesty, I couldn't. I'm sorry, but I feared you would regret the choice had I followed your orders."

"You have made a grave mistake." And from her belt she took out her dagger and slipped it into his gut, then twisted it violently. He fell to the ground as she pulled it out, blood dripping from the dagger. His blood felt warm. She looked at her hands for a moment, and then at the man who was writhing in agony on the stable floor. She should stab him again, she thought, to finish the deed. But then the blood dripping from the dagger caught her eye. Red and glistening.

Shiny.

Like an apple.

CHAPTER XXI

THE HAG AND
THE APPLE

The Queen went directly to her dungeon without a word to anyone she passed, her rage fuelling a supreme sense of power. She descended the winding stone staircase, and the chamber grew darker and darker as she descended. At the deepest depths of the dungeon was the room where she kept the sisters' books and practised the Black Arts. She slammed the dungeon door with a resounding clank.

"The heart of a pig! The blundering fool!" the Queen snapped.

The crow that had flown in months before

had remained there and was perched on a skull near the odd sisters' spell books. His wings fluttered as the Wicked Queen stormed about the dungeon.

The Queen decided that if she wanted Snow White dead, she must do it herself. But she was known far and wide. She would need to hide herself somehow if she were to travel over the Seven Jewelled Hills, beyond the seventh waterfall to Snow White. She darted over to the shelf where she kept the sisters' volumes on all kinds of magic: the Black Arts, witchcraft, alchemy, poisons... *disguises.*

She removed the large dusty old book, and set it upon a table. She would transform her regal, queenly appearance into that of an old pedlar woman. She flipped impatiently through the stained, tattered pages until she found the one labelled "Pedlar's Disguise."

The Queen prepared her beakers and set her potions to a boil. Then, carefully following the instructions set forth in the recipe for the potion, she added a pinch of mummy dust, to make herself old, followed by other ingredients to shroud her beautiful clothes, to age her voice and to whiten her hair.

When the formula was complete, she poured it into a crystal goblet and raised it to an open window where it was mixed well by the fierce wind and elements. She raised the glass to her lips and drank.

She had never mixed such a powerful potion and she had never felt a sensation like this before. The room began to spin, and the Queen was sure she would die. Colours swirled all around her, and she grasped her throat, which felt as if it were closing up. Then her hands began to tingle. She held them out before her and looked at them. They began to transform, withering into bony old hands with clawlike fingers.

Her throat began to burn. "My voice!" she said. But the voice that issued from her was not regal and bold, it was cracked and hoarse.

After a while the strange sensation subsided.

She gazed into a well-polished beaker and caught sight of her reflection. She was a haggard old woman like the one from her dream. Her chin was sharp. A wart adorned the tip of her hooked nose. Her eyebrows had grown thick, black and bushy. And her ragged yellow-grey hair blew into her face as the wind ushered through the window grate. Her clothes, too, had changed.

She was no longer dressed in her regal gown, but in an old black sackcloth with a hood to cover her ratty hair. She was the antithesis of everything she had been. A perfect disguise.

She could not help but laugh to herself. And now she would formulate a special sort of death for one so fair. What would it be? She felt around in her cloak, which still contained the apple Snow White had brought her. A poisoned apple! The Queen remembered back to when Snow White was a child, and the tale she told the Queen in which the sisters had mentioned enchanted fruit.

She flipped frantically through the sisters' book of potions and found it at last. One taste of the poisoned apple and the victim's eyes would close forever in the Sleeping Death. The Queen rummaged through the vials and canisters that were stored about the dungeon. She filled her cauldron with a healthy amount of skunk stock, and then added the rest of the formula, mostly herbs like foxglove and wolfsbane, with a dash of things much less ordinary, things found in mortuaries rather than forests.

Before long, her cauldron was bubbling with a green-grey liquid. The Queen considered the apple and smiled. Then she tied a thread around its stem so that she would be able to lower it into the elixir without touching the deadly potion. All she need do now, according to the sisters' book, was recite the incantation and lower the apple into the cauldron. Then the spell would be complete.

"Dip the apple in the brew, let the Sleeping Death seep through!" she recited.

And with that, she dipped the apple into the cauldron. When she did so, the green liquid turned a sickly blue, and as the now-black apple emerged from its bath, an ominous mark appeared upon it, the death's-head. This was confirmation that the spell was a success, just as the sisters' book said it would be. She need only recite one more incantation, and the spell would be sealed. "Now turn *red* to tempt Snow White, to make her hunger for a bite!"

The apple quickly turned from black to the brightest red the Queen had ever seen. She threw her head back and cackled insanely. She was well-armed now. But then she hesitated. What if there were an antidote? She rushed back to the sisters' book and flipped frantically through the pages. Yes, there was an antidote, the victim of the Sleeping Death could be awakened, but only by Love's First Kiss. For a moment the Queen was crestfallen and enraged. After all, the Prince would be searching for Snow White. What if he found her, lying there, and kissed her corpse in sorrow? She would awaken. The Wicked Queen quickly put the thought out of her mind. There would be no chance of that. Snow White was in the forest with the Seven Dwarfs.

They would find her body and think she was dead. And they would bury the girl *alive*.

The Queen laughed, startling the crow that inhabited the dungeon.

The Wicked Queen had only one thing left to do; deliver the apple.

She would soon once again be fairest of all.

CHAPTER XXII

THE CRONE, THE CLEARING AND THE COTTAGE

The Queen packed the poison apple in a basketful of others. It was the sole red one, so that she would be able to identify it when the time came to use it. She gathered up the basket and lifted a trapdoor in the dungeon. She descended the hidden staircase that led to an underground passage, where long ago the King had helped the Queen and Snow to make a hasty and unseen exit from the castle during an attack.

She hopped into the boat and rowed it down the underground river, which eventually opened up onto the castle moat, and finally into the swampland surrounding the forest.

It was still dead of night, and she was sure that she had gone unnoticed, a testament, she thought, to how poorly the castle guards did their job.

The Queen sneaked through the swampland and out into the forest towards the Seven Jewelled Hills. But with her new form, a hunched body and aching joints, it was not easy to navigate the uneven landscape, and she needed to stop often to rest.

And then she came to a clearing that was bathed in what little moonlight had been able to penetrate the clouds.

"Going off to do the deed then?" she heard a voice.

"Who is there?" the Queen asked, still not used to her own newly crotchety voice.

Three figures stepped from the shadows.

"You!" the Queen gasped.

"You have chosen the right path," the sisters said.

The Wicked Queen pushed them out of the way

and proceeded, limping deeper into the forest. She had what she needed: their spells and their potions. She had no further use for them.

"We hope you fare well," the sisters called after her as she continued her trek towards the Seven Jewelled Hills.

It was after dawn before she finally reached them. She listened for the roar of the seven falls, and followed their path. She carefully avoided wild beasts and creatures of the night. She was forced to climb over felled trees in order to cross roaring rivers and streams which, in her fragile state was not easy. But her determination was so strong, her will to kill Snow White so great, that she managed to arrive at the Seven Jewelled Hills. And just beyond them lay the cottage of the Seven Dwarfs, and in it, Snow White.

The Queen stood as tall as she could atop the hill and surveyed the landscape below. She noticed a worn little path that led into the woods. Chimney smoke hung over the treetops near where she suspected the path ended.

The Queen threw back her head and laughed

madly. Then she set out to follow the path.

She was soon rewarded for her efforts. The Queen stood behind a tree and watched the little house. The door opened and the little men the Slave had spoken of set off for their daily work in the mines.

And then, she saw her, Snow White!

The girl had came to the door and saw each of the men off. The Queen was disgusted and filled with venom and hatred. Onyx hair, lips like rubies, skin like snow, heart of gold... bah! The Queen knew better. Snow White was a selfish wench who cared nothing for her father's memory and was plotting to surpass her mother in the only thing the woman had left in this world, her beauty.

The Queen watched as the men left the house. The sun was streaming through the canopy of bird-filled tree branches. Snow White proceeded to the garden, where she fed bread crumbs to bluebirds. The Queen peeked from behind the tree where she was hiding; her clawlike fingers wrapped around a low branch and made a sickening scratching sound as she dug her nails into the bark of the tree, wishing it were Snow White's flesh.

"Hasn't changed one little bit," she whispered to herself in her new raspy voice.

She waited for Snow to go inside before she approached the cottage. She saw her in the open window, happily at work making pies.

The Queen quickly and suddenly thrust her head into the open window.

"All alone, my pet?" she asked.

Snow looked up from her work, clearly spooked by the sudden appearance of an old woman before her.

"Why, yes, I am, but—" the sweet girl answered.

"The little men are not here?" the Queen asked.

"No, they're not," Snow replied.

The Queen leaned forward and sniffed around the cottage.

"Making pies?" she asked.

"Yes, gooseberry pies."

Sweet.

Sickening.

Time to die.

"It's apple pies that makes the menfolk's mouths water," the Queen said. "Pies made from apples like *this*!"

She pulled the brilliant red apple from her basket and showed it to Snow White. The girl was hesitant, but the Queen used every persuasive bone in her frail old body to convince her to take a bite. Snow White looked enraptured by the apple, and she reached out to take it and pull it close to her lips.

Then suddenly, the Queen found herself attacked by what felt like a hoard of bats. But they couldn't be bats, it was mid-morning. She felt the creatures pecking at her and swatting her with their wings, talons tearing at her skin, and vicious beaks reaching hungrily for her eyes. She was lashed by feathers.

Birds!

She was being attacked by flocks of them. She raised her arms to block them and dropped the apple.

Snow White quickly came to her rescue, emerging from the cottage and chasing the birds away. The Queen quickly grabbed for the apple and checked it to assure that it wasn't damaged in any way. Snow White came to her side and apologised, and the Queen seized the opportunity to be invited into the cottage by complaining of a weak heart and expressing the need to sit down.

Snow went over to the far side of the cottage to fetch the Queen some water, and as she did so, the Queen pulled out the apple and formulated her plan. Then something unexpected... She couldn't do this to her little bird. Her heart ached.

Weakness.

Shove it away!

She buried the impulse deep within herself along with her grief, and focused on the matter at hand.

"And because you've been so good to poor old Granny, I'll share a secret with you. This is no ordinary apple. It's a magic wishing apple," the Queen said.

"A wishing apple?" Snow White asked.

The Queen got up from her seat and started moving towards Snow White with the apple extended before her.

"Yes! One bite and all your dreams will come true."

"Really?"

The Queen moved in closer.

"Yes. Now make a wish and take a bite…"

Snow looked apprehensive, and began to back away as the Queen advanced towards her with the apple extended.

"There must be *something* your little heart desires. Perhaps there's someone you love?" the Queen asked.

"Well, there is someone…" Snow replied.

"Ah! I thought so, I thought so," the Queen said, laughing. "Old Granny knows a young girl's heart. Now, take the apple, dearie, and make a wish."

The Queen thrust the apple into Snow White's hands. She smiled and nodded in encouragement as she watched the girl consider the apple.

Then the girl wished. She wished for all the things the Queen once had. For love, for a handsome prince to ride in on horseback and carry her away to his castle to make her his wife. But she also wished for something the Queen knew she herself could never have, and that was to live happily ever after.

The Queen watched, wringing her hands in anticipation.

"Quick! Don't let the wish grow cold!" she said.

And with that, Snow White sunk her teeth into the most beautiful, ripest apple she had ever seen.

"Oh, I feel strange," she said.

The Queen watched in anticipation as the effects of the poison set in. Snow wavered to and fro. The Queen rubbed her hands together and rocked back and forth... waiting. Waiting until she would again be fairest of all. And then, finally, Snow White fell to the ground. The bitten apple rolled from her hand, and the wicked Wicked Queen burst into maniacal laughter that could be heard throughout the kingdom. As if in response, a loud thunderclap resounded from above, and the sky opened up with a shower of pouring rain.

CHAPTER XXIII

THE CLIFF

Snow White lay at the Queen's feet as the old woman cackled. She thought she would be elated. Energized. Filled with joy. But instead, she felt weak. The long journey had taxed her. If only she wasn't stuck in this wretched old body! It would take her ages to get back to the castle. She wanted nothing more than to ask the mirror who was now fairest of all.

She hadn't bothered to see what she needed to reverse the Pedlar's Disguise potion. Surely the sisters had something tucked away in that old trunk they left.

"Apologies, my Queen." It was one of the

sisters' voices, though the woman was nowhere to be seen.

"There is no antidote," another voice echoed, followed by the sisters' odd chattering laughter.

Panic.

"No antidote! No way to reverse it? Impossible. There has to be a way!" She mentally flipped through the pages of the old book, her heart pounding, hands shaking; she had to sit down again, her heart was that of an old woman.

"Calm yourself," she said.

Her head was spinning, and she couldn't catch her breath. "All for nothing!" She felt numb. She couldn't face her father's reflection in the mirror like this. Old, ugly, worthless. And then she found herself doing the only thing she could. The Queen broke into hysterical laughter. Her life, this day, it had all been so ridiculous. How had she come to this point? She could not control her laughter and she cackled loudly as she stepped out of the door into the rain. Perhaps it would cleanse her. Renew her. Give her some perspective.

She had hated her father and then become just like him. Heartless. Wicked. Cruel. She made a ruin of her life for nothing. She would never be the fairest, not like this. Nothing! She had killed her little bird for nothing. Her head was splitting with pain, she was thrown, taken aback by her guilt, her regret. But what did she regret most, the ruin of Snow's life or her own?

Suddenly, the little men came crashing into the garden, they'd known what had happened and were crying out for the Queen's death. The shock jolted her out of any sentimental reverie, and she was once again wicked, now concerned only with preserving her own life.

She scrambled to her feet and ran as fast as she could. The men looked nothing like she had imagined. Their faces screwed up in anger, they knew why she was there, they knew what she had done; somehow, these men possessed a magic of their own.

She ran from the men in a panic, her heart racing and terror gripping at her. Her strides much wider than theirs, she had managed to gain a fair amount of distance on the tiny men, even running in the pouring rain in her weakened state.

The men did not relent, and they pursued her into the forest. Still, she maintained her lead on them.

And then she came to a split in the path. One path led up a cliff, at the top of which was a huge boulder. The other continued farther into the woods. If she ran into the woods, perhaps she could lose herself among the trees. If she ran up to the top of the cliff, she would be trapped.

And then, the sisters appeared again.

"My Queen, we can guarantee that taking the path that leads to the boulder will mean certain death for you."

The sisters were more serious than the Queen had ever heard them before. Their voices were devoid of eerie laughter.

"We implore you, take to the forest. You will be safe there. We can find you and reverse the hag spell. Forgive our dishonesty…"

The Queen considered her options. The forest,

safety. A haven for her. A new chance at life.

But what kind of life? She thought back to the day she had met the King at the well. She remembered how warm his hands felt on hers, how she had never been touched that way before, how no one had ever loved her, *ever*. Her wedding day came to mind, the joy she had felt and that which emanated from every corner of the kingdom, nay, all the lands.

And then there was Snow White… Ah, she loved the child. She loved her as the daughter she was by right of marriage. So beautiful and pure. Such a precocious little one. A real beauty who loved the King and honoured his memory by living life in full even after his death. Unlike the Queen who allowed treachery, pain and vanity to destroy her. She remembered holding Snow when she told her the King had been killed… and the Apple Blossom Festival, and all those days with Verona, and all the picnics and breakfasts in the morning room.

The Queen had had so much promise within her; so much power to make the world better. But instead she allowed darkness to guide her, blind to any other way.

The men were now close behind her. The sisters had again vanished.

The Queen glanced at the cliff as the clouds battered her with rain and the sky whipped at her with lightning lashes. She looked up and she knew what she needed to do.

After all, she had chosen her path long ago.

Epilogue

Snow White blinked her eyes and woke to Love's First Kiss.

She felt weary and odd, but ecstatic. Her Prince had come. He had broken the spell. He had saved her. Perhaps the old crone's apple was truly magical after all, for Snow White's wishes had come true.

The two were married soon after, and on the night of their wedding the trees were filled with fireflies blinking in the darkness. The sky was full of glittering starlight, like shards from broken mirrors scattered over the ocean. The castle was decorated with her favourite flowers, the scent bringing back lovely memories. Snow danced with her husband in the great hall, imagining her mothers dancing with her, smiling, and wishing her well as the Queen's mirrored cylinder spun, casting gorgeous patterns on the stone walls. She kissed her Prince.

Bliss.

Snow White held her Prince's hand, wondering what her new life would be like. With her stepmother gone, she was now queen of her kingdom. And she thought she would rule as justly and passionately as her father had, and as her stepmother might have if things had been different.

She kissed her Prince again and looked to the stars, feeling a sense of love she'd never felt before.

She was happy.

The only thing she longed for that day was her father and mothers. She had lost them when she was very young, at least that is how she thought of it. No one understood why she still loved the Queen. But to Snow, her stepmother had died the day her father was killed, and up until that day the woman had been a guardian angel to her.

Later that evening, alone in her chamber, after a long day of wedding festivities, Snow White noticed that her chambermaid had piled some of the wedding gifts next to her fireplace. She curled up in an overstuffed velvet chair, tucking her feet to one side and suddenly feeling very small, like a little bird.

Little bird. That is what her stepmother used to call her.

How she wished she were here now. How she wished she hadn't been destroyed by her vanity and grief. She dragged one of the larger packages from beside the bed and tore it open.

It was her mother's favourite mirror. The one she looked upon obsessively.

Snow White was taken aback as the glass filled with lapping flames, followed by a swirl of mist.

Epilogue

And then a face appeared.

"I love you, my beautiful little bird," said the Queen from the Magic Mirror. "I always have and I always will."

The Queen blew the girl a kiss.

And Snow White smiled.

THE END